IMMIGRANT

Why the Kimonians allowed Earth to send its people was a mystery for which there was no answer. But apparently Earth was the only planet in the galaxy which had been allowed to send its people. The Earthmen and the Kimonians, of course, were both humanoid, but this was not an adequate answer, either, for they were not the only humanoids in the galaxy. For its own comfort Earth assumed that a certain common understanding, a similar outlook, a certain parallel evolutionary trend – with Earth a bit behind of course – between Earth and Kimon might account for Kimon's qualified hospitality.

Be that as it may, Kimon was galactic El Dorado, a never-never land, a place to get ahead, the place to spend your life, the country at the rainbow's end.

By the same author
in Mandarin Paperbacks

Clifford D. Simak

IMMIGRANT
and other stories

*Collected and with an introduction
by Francis Lyall*

Mandarin

A Mandarin Paperback

IMMIGRANT AND OTHER STORIES

First published in Great Britain 1991
by Mandarin Paperbacks
Michelin House, 81 Fulham Road, London SW3 6RB

Mandarin is an imprint of the Octopus Publishing Group,
a division of Reed International Books Limited.

Introduction Copyright © Francis Lyall 1991

'Neighbor' copyright © Street and Smith Publications 1954
Copyright © Clifford D. Simak 1982

'Green Thumb' copyright © Galaxy Publishing Corp., 1954
Copyright © Clifford D. Simak 1982

'Small Deer' copyright © Galaxy Publishing House, 1965

'The Ghost of a Model T' copyright © 1975, Robert Silverberg and Roger Elwood, eds,
Epoch, New York: Berkeley Publishing Corp./G. P. Putnam's Sons 1975

'Byte Your Tongue!' copyright © Random House Inc., 1980

'I Am Crying All Inside' copyright © Galaxy Publishing Corp., 1969

'Immigrant' copyright © Street and Smith Publications, 1954
Copyright © Clifford D. Simak 1982

A CIP catalogue record for this title
is available from the British Library
ISBN 0 7493 0644 0

Printed and bound in Great Britain
by Cox & Wyman Ltd, Reading, Berks

Contents

INTRODUCTION

Though there are many arguments over the literary history of science fiction, it is incontrovertible that the master sf writers of this century have produced a body of work which has fascinated successive generations of readers. Some stand pre-eminent even among the masters, and such a one is my friend Clifford D. Simak. Each of the major sf authors have a hall-mark of individuality that distinguishes them. The 'flavour' of Clarke, Asimov, Heinlein or Leinster, of Le Guin, McCaffery or Cherryh, depends upon a variety of factors – typical setting, pace, language, use of science and plot, to name but a few. The work of Clifford D. Simak also shows such strong identifying characteristics.

CDS was a newspaperman for the bulk of his long working life. Despite a very busy professional life he published over two hundred stories and twenty-seven novels, some of them classics, *City* of 1952 and *Way Station* of 1963 being perhaps the best known at novel length. His awards and nominations from the sf writing and the sf reading communities include three Hugo's (for 'The Big Front Yard', 1959; *Way Station*, 1964; and 'The Grotto of the Dancing Deer', 1980) and a Nebula (for 'The Grotto of the Dancing Deer', 1980 – which also won the Locus short story award for that year). In 1977 he received the Nebula Grand Master award of the Science Fiction Writers of

America as well as the Jupiter Award (for *A Heritage of Stars*, 1977), and in 1953 he was awarded the International Fantasy Award for *City*. He retired in 1976, but kept on writing. His last novel was *Highway of Eternity* (1986). He died in April 1988.

Although much of his life was spent in the offices of first the Minneapolis *Star* and then the Minneapolis *Tribune*, no one can doubt that CDS was formed by his early life in the rural communities of south-west Wisconsin. He was born on his grandfather's farm, which still lies on the ridge country of Millville Township high on the bluffs of the south bank of the Wisconsin as it flows its last miles to the Mississippi. His father's farm is the next to the east on the same ridge on the south side of the road, and the 'stone house' which his father built still looks out over to Prairie du Chien at the end of the road, one farm past his grandfather's farm with its 'Whistling Well'.

CDS grew up in that farming country, was educated at Patch Grove, and for some years taught school in other small towns in the area, including Glen Haven. His wife, Kay, was a lassie from Cassville, the next town down the river from Glen Haven. That triangle of country, Grant County, Wisconsin, bounded to the north by the last few miles of the Wisconsin and to the west by the Mississippi, can truly be called 'Simak Country', the country of his imagination, just as Hardy had his Wessex and Faulkner his Yoknapatawpha County. Nor do these comparisons take CDS out of his league – out of fashion, perhaps, but not league.

The scenes and scenery of his childhood, youth and young manhood, as well as its manners, expectations and morality, make frequent appearance in CDS's works. The old grey *Way Station*, for example, is set there, high above the river, and Enoch Wallace walks familiar ridges and valleys. The example is not isolated. Much of the action of such novels as *Why Call Them Back from Heaven* (1967), and *Ring Around the Sun* (1953) lies in such areas. In *Time and Again* (1951, aka *First He Died*), the hero escapes back down time to just such a farm as CDS's to take refuge. Nor

8

is it only the novels that show such affection for bluff and ridge country. CDS's short stories often take place in the region of his upbringing. That has been plain in earlier collections, for example in the title story of *The Marathon Photograph* (Severn House, 1986, Methuen, 1987), and in 'The Whistling Well' in that book. Several of the stories in *Brother* (Severn House, 1986, Methuen, 1988) are similarly located. This selection is no different.

Take topography first. 'The Ghost of a Model T' is full of Simak country. It is firmly placed in the ridge farming country with its winding roads and small communities. Willow Bend, Hank's village, is a location CDS uses often in his tales, and indeed it appears also in 'Small Deer' in this collection. 'Willow Bend' is always a subtle amalgam of Millville, the main village of the township of CDS's birth, and other communities along the Wisconsin and the Mississippi. There are other clear Grant County referents in 'Ghost'. A high road does run more or less straight along the ridge above the river before dipping to meet a road that runs beside the willows of the Wisconsin east from the Highway 18 bridge at Bridgeport. I have driven both the high and the river road. The Model T bears Hank to the Big Spring Pavilion. I asked CDS's brother Carson about this and when I visited in September 1990 he took me to the site. 'Spring' does not refer to the season, but the Big Spring lying just off the old Highway 18 just before it ends the slow rise from the river and turns east and Highway 133 branches south to Patch Grove. The Pavilion is long gone. Highway 18 has been realigned and the Spring culverted. But back in Prohibition days the Pavilion was a well-known rendezvous for young folk, for dancers, and for the bootleggers. Just as in Hank's case, if you left the Pavilion temporarily your readmission was secured by an inky stamp on the back of the hand.

Other of the stories show similar traces. In 'Green Thumb' Joe lives in his old family homestead; one of his clients lives out on Acorn Ridge. Having driven round CDS's childhood scenes, I am pretty sure I could take you there.

Another favourite CDS place, Coon Valley, is a lovely valley with sweeping side-valleys and well-kept farms. The real Coon Valley is almost an hour's drive north from the Wisconsin on the Viroqua to La Crosse highway, Highway 14/61. Towards the top of the valley is the village of Coon Valley itself. 'Coon Valley' and 'Coon Creek' recur in CDS stories and he acknowledged that the real valley was a major stimulus to his imagination. The imaginary Coon Valley is a cross between the real one and the smaller, poorer valleys of the ridge country CDS knew so well. In 'Neighbor' the first words place the story in yet another Coon Valley, and the story itself is shot through with understanding of such valleys and the people that live there.

Last, topographically, there is 'Small Deer'. In form this story is a letter written from yet another 'Willow Bend, Wisconsin' to Dr Jackson at Wyalusing College, Muscoda. Muscoda is upstream on the Wisconsin on the river road already mentioned. Drive west along that road from the Bridgeport Bridge, and you arrive at Wyalusing State Park set high on the bluffs overlooking the marshes that form the estuary of the Wisconsin. The geology surrounding 'Small Deer's Willow Bend is crucial for time travel for the reasons given in the letter. Platteville limestone is a real phenomenon. Platteville limestone forms much of the bluffs on which CDS's parents' and grand-parents' farms lie, the Platteville plate underlying much of Grant County. The region has never been glaciated, and therefore allows time travel without the problem of changed elevations. For that reason it appears in a number of CDS's other 'time' tales (for example, *Mastodonia* (1978), 'The Thing in the Stone' and 'The Marathon Photograph'). It also produces wonderful sites for flowers as Cliff occasionally mentions in many stories.

But it is not just the land of his childhood and youth that recur in CDS's work. The people do too. The caring and underlying respect for traditional ways and moral values that suffuse most of the stories, derive from rural community life. It is these elements that make most of

CDS's tales readily identifiable as his. Often there is also some admixture of nostalgia — but it is always clear and well-distilled, a healthy nostalgia, not the too prevalent mawkish, synthetic brand of some of today's writers. In this collection 'The Ghost of a Model T' has the highest nostalgia quotient. CDS himself reckoned this story closer to the spirit of the 1920s than all the books that have been written about it. Certainly the tale carries a flavour which others can only attempt to describe, not to evoke.

Nostalgia is also present in 'Neighbor', the nostalgia of a farm boy who has gone to the city, as Cliff did. But here note the good humour. 'Neighbor' is a story written by a working newspaperman: see what happens in it to a newspaperman! See also how the value of the slower, perhaps more genuine life of country places is indicated. That is unusual in sf, a genre which is more often city-based and frenetic, urban not urbane. In most sf the individual fights and struggles, the morality is self-seeking and the hero possessed of super-human qualities (I say nothing of the new anti-hero vogue). By contrast CDS's heroes are clearly individuals, individuals with defects, but with a propensity in the last analysis to do what is right rather than what is expedient: and often that brings what Tolkien called a *eucatastrophe*, a happy outcome that retrospectively suffuses the tale with warmth.

CDS's respect for individuals always extended beyond the human. Occasionally his stories feature vegetable life. 'Green Thumb', first published in 1954, may be an early foreshadowing of thinking kindly at your pot-plants. And as in many CDS stories, he who acts kindly is repaid in unlooked-for ways.

CDS's robots are also typical of him. They linger in the mind. Jenkins of *City* and Enoch, Cardinal Theodosius of *Project Pope* (1981) need only be named. Here, we have the dreaming computer, Fred of 'Byte your Tongue!'. It is unusual for CDS to give such a prosaic name to the computer but that enhances the story. Fred dreams, is induced to commit folly and is punished: and yet, the story suggests, perhaps that dreaming was not ineffective.

11

That point could be analogised to sf in general. Sf dreamers have had effects. Look around you!

But I would not give the impression that CDS depicted nothing but sweetness and light. 'Byte your Tongue!' contains a stark contrast between Fred on the one side and the Senator and his aide on the other. CDS was fascinated by Congressional affairs and at one time he would have liked to have gone to Washington. His interest is seen, and his trenchant comment on some of the goings-on of the 1980s is foreshadowed, in what happens to Senator Moore and Daniel Waite. Given the 1970s and 80s the fitness monitoring system contained within the tale is an intriguing notion.

If 'Byte your Tongue!' indicates an awareness of the seamier, less pleasant elements of life, what of 'I Am Crying All Inside'? What also of 'Small Deer'? Perhaps a meteor was responsible for the end of the dinosaurs, but perhaps not: and if not, might the now teeming population of Earth not be cheap protein just awaiting culling?

Finally there is 'Immigrant'. In its ways it balances 'Neighbor', and is equally redolent of CDS themes. It was not until I was drafting the copyright information for this collection that I noticed that 'Immigrant' and 'Neighbor' were first published in the same magazine within months of each other. One can but assume that they were written reasonably close together, and that their mutual balancing is, if not deliberate, at least understandable as the conscious and unconscious mind of the tale-smith developed the stories. 'Immigrant' also echoes such as 'Kindergarten' in *Brother*. I would say little but 'read it'. Bishop, though highly intelligent, is nonetheless humble – a combination rare in modern life. As a result he eventually learns enough wisdom to understand, and, we assume, to profit from the studies that are to start next day. I read this story years and years ago, and it stuck somewhere at the back of my mind. It has helped.

And in that, CDS achieved an aim. He wrote first to entertain, but he was never blind to the possibility that his stories might influence and would recast and rewrite for that purpose. But he was an excellent story-smith, and the recasting almost never shows. He was conscious that stories pass into the psyche of their readers, and that a diet of immorality (taking that term at its widest) will damage personalities and trigger behavioural and other flaws. By contrast CDS's influence was for good – sometimes a disparaged quality, but one essential for civilisation. I hope you too enjoy and appreciate his work.

F. Lyall.

Aberdeen, Scotland.
May 1991.

NEIGHBOR

Coon Valley is a pleasant place, but there's no denying it's sort of off the beaten track and it's not a place where you can count on getting rich because the farms are small and a lot of the ground is rough. You can farm the bottom-lands, but the hillsides are only good for pasture and the roads are just dirt roads, impassable at certain times of year.

The old-timers, like Bert Smith and Jingo Harris and myself, are well satisfied to stay here, for we grew up with the country and we haven't any illusions about getting rich and we'd feel strange and out-of-place anywhere but in the valley. But there are others, newcomers, who move in and get discouraged after a while and up and move away, so there usually is a farm or two standing idle, waiting to be sold.

We are just plain dirt farmers, with emphasis on the dirt, for we can't afford a lot of fancy machinery and we don't go in for blooded stock – but there's nothing wrong with us; we're just everyday, the kind of people you meet all over these United States. Because we're out of the way and some of the families have lived here for so long, I suppose you could say that we have gotten clannish. But that doesn't mean we don't like outside folks; it just means we've lived so long together that we've got to know and

15

like one another and are satisfied with things just as they are.

We have radios, of course, and we listen to the programs and the news, and some of us take daily papers, but I'm afraid that we may be a bit provincial, for it's fairly hard to get us stirred up much about world happenings. There's so much of interest right here in the valley we haven't got the time to worry about all those outside things. I imagine you'd call us conservative, for most of us vote Republican without even wondering why and there's none of us who has much time for all this government interference in the farming business.

The valley has always been a pleasant place – not only the land, but the people in it, and we've always been fortunate in the new neighbors that we get. Despite new ones coming in every year or so, we've never had a really bad one and that means a lot to us.

But we always worry a little when one of the new ones up and moves away and we speculate among ourselves, wondering what kind of people will buy or rent the vacant farm.

The old Lewis farm had been abandoned for a long time, the buildings all run down and gone to ruin and the fields gone back to grass. A dentist over at Hopkins Corners had rented it for several years and run some cattle in it, driving out on week-ends to see how they were doing. We used to wonder every now and then if anyone would ever farm the place again, but finally we quit wondering, for the buildings had fallen into such disrepair that we figured no one ever would. I went in one day and talked to the banker at Hopkins Corners, who had the renting of the place, and told him I'd like to take it over if the dentist ever gave it up. But he told me the owners, who lived in Chicago then, were anxious to sell rather than to rent it, although he didn't seem too optimistic that anyone would buy it.

Then one spring a new family moved onto the farm and in time we learned it had been sold and that the new family's name was Heath – Reginald Heath. And Bert

Smith said to me: 'Reginald! That's a hell of a name for a farmer!' But that was all he said.

Jingo Harris stopped by one day, coming home from town, when he saw Heath out in the yard, to pass the time of day. It was a neighborly thing to do, of course, and Heath seemed glad to have him stop, although Jingo said he seemed to be a funny kind of man to be a farmer.

'He's a foreigner,' Jingo told me. 'Sort of dark. Like he might be a Spaniard or from one of those other countries. I don't know how he got that Reginald. Reginald is English and Heath's no Englishman.'

Later on we heard that the Heaths weren't really Spanish, but were Rumanians or Bulgarians and that they were refugees from the Iron Curtain.

But Spanish, or Rumanian, or Bulgarian, the Heaths were workers. There was Heath and his wife and a half-grown girl and all three of them worked all the blessed time. They paid attention to their business and didn't bother anyone and because of this we liked them, although we didn't have much to do with them. Not that we didn't want to or that they didn't want us to; it's just that in a community like ours new folks sort of have to grow in instead of being taken in.

Heath had an old beaten-up wired-together tractor that made a lot of noise, and as soon as the soil was dry enough to plow he started out to turn over the fields that through the years had grown up to grass. I used to wonder if he worked all night long, for many times when I went to bed I heard the tractor running. Although that may not be as late as it sounds to city dwellers, for here in the valley we go to bed early – and get up early, too.

One night after dark I set out to hunt some cows, a couple of fence-jumping heifers that gave me lots of trouble. Just let a man come in late from work and tired and maybe it's raining a little and dark as the inside of a cat and those two heifers would turn up missing and I'd have to go and hunt them. I tried all the different kinds of pokes and none of them did any good. When a heifer gets to fence-jumping there isn't much that can be done with her.

So I lit a lantern and set out to hunt for them, but I hunted for two hours and didn't find a trace of them. I had just about decided to give up and go back home when I heard the sound of a tractor running and realized that I was just above the west field of the old Lewis place. To get home I'd have to go right past the field and I figured it might be as well to wait when I reached the field until the tractor came around and ask Heath if he had seen the heifers.

It was a dark night, with thin clouds hiding the stars and a wind blowing high in the treetops and there was a smell of rain in the air. Heath, I figured, probably was staying out extra late to finish up the field ahead of the coming rain, although I remember that I thought he was pushing things just a little hard. Already he was far ahead of all the others in the valley with his plowing.

So I made my way down the steep hillside and waded the creek at a shallow place I knew and while I was doing this I heard the tractor make a complete round of the field. I looked for the headlight, but I didn't see it and I thought probably the trees had hidden it from me.

I reached the edge of the field and climbed through the fence, walking out across the furrows to intercept the tractor. I heard it make the turn to the east of me and start down the field toward me and although I could hear the noise of it, there wasn't any light.

I found the last furrow and stood there waiting, sort of wondering, not too alarmed as yet, how Heath managed to drive the rig without any light. I thought that maybe he had cat eyes and could see in the dark and although it seemed funny later when I remembered it, the idea that a man might have cat eyes did not seem funny then.

The noise kept getting louder and it seemed to be coming pretty close, when all at once the tractor rushed out of the dark and seemed to leap at me. I guess I must have been afraid that it would run over me, for I jumped back a yard or two, with my heart up in my neck. But I needn't have bothered, for I was out of the way to start with.

The tractor went on past me and I waved the lantern and yelled for Heath to stop and as I waved the lantern the light was thrown onto the rear of the tractor and I saw there was no one on it.

A hundred things went through my mind, but the one idea that stuck was that Heath had fallen off the tractor and might be lying injured, somewhere in the field.

I ran after the tractor, thinking to shut it down before it got loose and ran into a tree or something, but by the time I reached it, it had reached a turn and it was making that turn as neatly as if it had been broad daylight and someone had been driving it.

I jumped up on the drawbar and grabbed the seat, hauling myself up. I reached out a hand, grabbing for the throttle, but with my hand upon the metal I didn't pull it back. The tractor had completed the turn now and was going down the furrow – and there was something else.

Take an old tractor, now – one that wheezed and coughed and hammered and kept threatening to fall apart, like this one did – and you are bound to get a lot of engine vibration. But in this tractor there was no vibration. It ran along as smooth as a high-priced car and the only jolts you got were when the wheels hit a bump or slight gully in the field.

I stood there, hanging onto the lantern with one hand and clutching the throttle with the other, and I didn't do a thing. I just rode down to the point where the tractor started to make another turn. Then I stepped off and went on home. I didn't hunt for Heath lying in the field, for I knew he wasn't there.

I suppose I wondered how it was possible, but I didn't really fret myself too much trying to figure it all out. I imagine, in the first place, I was just too numb. You may worry a lot about little things that don't seem quite right, but when you run into a big thing, like that self-operating tractor, you sort of give up automatically, knowing that it's too big for your brain to handle, that it's something you haven't got a chance of solving. And after a while you forget it because it's something you can't live with. So your mind rejects it.

I got home and stood out in the barnyard for a moment, listening. The wind was blowing fairly hard by then and the first drops of rain were falling, but every now and then, when the wind would quiet down, I could hear the tractor.

I went inside the house and Helen and the kids were all in bed and sound asleep, so I didn't say anything about it that night. And the next morning, when I had a chance to think about it, I didn't say anything at all. Mostly, I suppose, because I knew no one would believe me and that I'd have to take a lot of kidding about automatic tractors.

Heath got his plowing done and his crops in, well ahead of everyone in the valley. The crops came up in good shape and we had good growing weather; then along in June we got a spell of wet, and everyone got behind with corn plowing because you can't go out in the field when the ground is soggy. All of us chored around our places, fixing fences and doing other odd jobs, cussing out the rain and watching the weeds grow like mad in the unplowed field.

All of us, that is, except Heath. His corn was clean as a whistle and you had to hunt to find a weed. Jingo stopped by one day and asked him how he managed, but Heath just laughed a little, in that quiet way of his, and talked of something else.

The first apples finally were big enough for green-apple pies and there is no one in the country makes better green-apple pies than Helen. She wins prizes with her pies every year at the county fair and she is proud of them.

One day she wrapped up a couple of pies and took them over to the Heaths. It's a neighborly way we have of doing in the valley, with the women running back and forth from one neighbor to another with their cooking. Each one of them has some dish she likes to show off to the neighbors and it's a sort of harmless way of bragging.

Helen and the Heaths got along just swell. She was late in getting home and I was starting supper, with the kids yelling they were hungry when-do-we-eat-around-here, when she finally showed up.

She was full of talk about the Heaths – how they had fixed up the house, you never would have thought anyone could do so much to such a terribly run-down place as they had, and about the garden they had – especially about the garden. It was a big one, she said, and beautifully taken care of and it was full of vegetables she had never seen before. The funniest things you ever saw, she said. Not the ordinary kind of vegetables.

We talked some about those vegetables, speculating that maybe the Heaths had brought the seeds out with them from behind the Iron Curtain, although so far as I could remember, vegetables were vegetables, no matter where you were. They grew the same things in Russia or Rumania or Timbuktu as we did. And, anyhow, by this time I was getting a little skeptical about that story of their escaping from Rumania.

But we didn't have the time for much serious speculation on the Heaths, although there was plenty of casual gossip going around the neighborhood. Haying came along and then the small-grain harvest and everyone was busy. The hay was good and the small-grain crop was fair, but it didn't look like we'd get much corn. For we hit a drought. That's the way it goes – too much rain in June, not enough in August.

We watched the corn and watched the sky and felt hopeful when a cloud showed up, but the clouds never meant a thing. It just seems at times that God isn't on your side.

Then one morning Jingo Harris showed up and stood around, first on one foot, then the other, talking to me while I worked on an old corn binder that was about worn out and which it didn't look nohow I'd need to use that year.

'Jingo,' I said, after I'd watched him fidget for an hour or more, 'you got something on your mind.'

He blurted it out then. 'Heath got rain last night,' he said.

'No one else did,' I told him.

'I guess you're right,' said Jingo. 'Heath's the only one.'

He told me how he'd gone to cut through Heath's north cornfield, carrying back a couple of balls of binder twine he'd borrowed from Bert Smith. It wasn't until he'd crawled through the fence that he noticed the field was wet, soaked by a heavy rain.

'It must have happened in the night,' he said.

He thought it was funny, but figured maybe there had been a shower across the lower end of the valley, although as a rule rains travel up and down the valley, not across it. But when he had crossed the corner of the field and crawled through the fence, he noticed it hadn't rained at all. So he went back and walked around the field and the rain had fallen on the field, but nowhere else. It began at the fence and ended at the fence.

When he'd made a circuit of the field he sat down on one of the balls of twine and tried to get it all thought out but it made no sense − furthermore, it was plain unbelievable.

Jingo is a thorough man. He likes to have all the evidence and know all there is to know before he makes up his mind. So he went over to Heath's second corn patch, on the west side of the valley. And once again, he found that it had rained on that field − on the field, but not around the field.

'What do you make of it?' Jingo asked me and I said I didn't know. I came mighty close to telling him about the unmanned tractor, but I thought better of it. After all, there was no point in getting the neighborhood stirred up.

After Jingo left I got in the car and drove over to the Heath farm, intending to ask him if he could loan me his posthole digger for a day or two. Not that I was going to dig any postholes, but you have to have some excuse for showing up at a neighbor's place.

I never got a chance to ask him for that posthole digger, though. Once I got there I never even thought of it.

Heath was sitting on the front steps of the porch and he seemed glad to see me. He came down to the car and shook my hand and said, 'It's good to see you, Calvin.' The way he said it made me feel friendly and sort of important, too – especially that Calvin business, for everyone else just calls me Cal. I'm not downright sure, in fact, that anyone in the neighborhood remembers that my name is Calvin.

'I'd like to show you around the place,' he said. 'We've done some fixing up.'

Fixing up wasn't exactly the word for it. The place was spic and span. It looked like some of those Pennsylvania and Connecticut farms you see in the magazines. The house and all the other buildings had been ramshackle with all the paint peeled off them and looking as if they might fall down at any minute. But now they had a sprightly, solid look and they gleamed with paint. They didn't look new, of course, but they looked as if they'd always been well taken care of and painted every year. The fences were all fixed up and painted, too, and the weeds were cut and a couple of old unsightly scrap-lumber piles had been cleaned up and burned. Heath had even tackled an old iron and machinery junk pile and had it sorted out.

'There was a lot to do,' said Heath, 'but I feel it's worth it. I have an orderly soul. I like to have things neat.'

Which might be true, of course, but he'd done it all in less than six months' time. He'd come to the farm in early March and it was only August and he'd not only put in some hundred acres of crops and done all the other farm work, but he'd got the place fixed up. And that wasn't possible, I told myself. One man couldn't do it, not even with his wife and daughter helping – not even if he worked twenty-four hours a day and didn't stop to eat. Or unless he could take time and stretch it out to make one hour equal three or four.

I trailed along behind Heath and thought about the time-stretching business and was pleased at myself for thinking of it, for it isn't often that I get foolish thoughts

23

that are likewise pleasing. Why, I thought, with a deal like that you could stretch out any day so you could get all the work done you wanted to. And if you could stretch out time, maybe you could compress it, too, so that a trip to a dentist, for example, would only seem to take a minute.

Heath took me out to the garden and Helen had been right. There were the familiar vegetables, of course — cabbages and tomatoes and squashes and all the other kinds that were found in every garden — but in addition to this there were as many others I had never seen before. He told me the names of them and they seemed to be queer names then, although now it seems a little strange to think they once had sounded queer, for now everyone in the valley grows these vegetables and it seems like we have always had them.

As we talked he pulled up and picked some of the strange vegetables and put them in a basket he had brought along.

'You'll want to try them all,' he said. 'Some of them you may not like at first, but there are others that you will. This one you eat raw, sliced like a tomato, and this one is best boiled, although you can bake it, too — '

I wanted to ask him how he'd come on the vegetables and where they had come from, but he didn't give me a chance; he kept on telling me about them and how to cook them and that this one was a winter keeper and that one you could can and he gave me one to eat raw and it was rather good.

We'd got to the far end of the garden and were starting to come back when Heath's wife ran around the corner of the house.

Apparently she didn't see me at first or had forgotten I was there, for she called to him and the name she called him wasn't Reginald or Reggie, but a foreign-sounding name. I won't even try to approximate it, for even at the time I wasn't able to recall it a second after hearing it. It was like no word I'd ever heard before.

Then she saw me and stopped running and caught her breath, and a moment later said she'd been listening in on the party line and that Bert Smith's little daughter, Ann, was terribly sick.

'They called the doctor,' she said, 'but he is out on calls and he won't get there in time.'

'Reginald,' she said, 'the symptoms sound like – '

And she said another name that was like none I'd ever heard or expect to hear again.

Watching Heath's face, I could swear I saw it pale despite his olive tinge of skin.

'Quick!' he shouted and grabbed me by the arm.

We ran around in front to his old clunk of a car. He threw the basket of vegetables in the back seat and jumped behind the wheel. I scrambled in after him and tried to close the door, but it wouldn't close. The lock kept slipping loose and I had to hang onto the door so it wouldn't bang.

We lit out of there like a turpentined dog and the noise that old car made was enough to deafen one. Despite my holding onto it, the door kept banging and all the fenders rattled and there was every other kind of noise you'd expect a junk-heap car to make, with an extra two or three thrown in.

I wanted to ask him what he planned to do, but I was having trouble framing the question in my mind and even if I had known how to phrase it I doubt he could have heard me with all the racket that the car was making.

So I hung on as best I could and tried to keep the door from banging and all at once it seemed to me the car was making more noise than it had any call to. Just like the old haywire tractor made more noise than any tractor should. Too much noise, by far, for the way that it was running. Just like on the tractor, there was no engine vibration and despite all the banging and the clanking we were making time. As I've said, our valley roads are none too good, but even so I swear there were places we hit seventy and we went around sharp corners where, by rights, we should have gone into the ditch at the speed that we were going, but the car just seemed to settle down and hug the road and we never even skidded.

25

We pulled up in front of Bert's place and Heath jumped out and ran up the walk, with me following him.

Amy Smith came to the door and I could see that she'd been crying, and she looked a little surprised to see the two of us.

We stood there for a moment without saying anything, then Heath spoke to her and here is a funny thing: Heath was wearing a pair of ragged overalls and a sweat-stained shirt and he didn't have a hat and his hair was all rumpled up, but there was a single instant when it seemed to me that he was well-dressed in an expensive business suit and that he took off his hat and bowed to Amy.

'I understand,' he said, 'that the little girl is sick. Maybe I can help.'

I don't know if Amy had seen the same thing that I had seemed to see, but she opened the door and stood to one side so that we could enter.

'In there,' she said.

'Thank you, ma'am,' said Heath, and went into the room.

Amy and I stood there for a moment, then she turned to me and I could see the tears in her eyes again.

'Cal, she's awful sick,' she said.

I nodded miserably, for now the spell was gone and common sense was coming back again and I wondered at the madness of this farmer who thought that he could help a little girl who was terribly sick. And at my madness for standing there, without even going in the room with him.

But just then Heath came out of the room and closed the door softly behind him.

'She's sleeping now,' he said to Amy. 'She'll be all right.'

Then, without another word, he walked out of the door. I hesitated a moment, looking at Amy, wondering what to do. And it was pretty plain there was nothing I could do. So I followed him.

We drove back to his farm at a sober rate of speed, but the car banged and thumped just as bad as ever.

'Runs real good,' I yelled at him.

He smiled at bit.

'I keep it tinkered up,' he yelled back at me.

When we got to his place, I got out of his car and walked over to my own.

'You forgot the vegetables,' he called after me.

So I went back to get them.

'Thanks a lot,' I said.

'Anytime,' he told me.

I looked straight at him, then, and said: 'It sure would be fine if we could get some rain. It would mean a lot to us. A soaking rain right now would save the corn.'

'Come again,' he told me. 'It was good to talk with you.'

And that night it rained, all over the valley, a steady, soaking rain, and the corn was saved.

And Ann got well.

The doctor, when he finally got to Bert's, said that she had passed the crisis and was already on the mend. One of those virus things, he said. A lot of it around. Not like the old days, he said, before they got to fooling around with all their miracle drugs, mutating viruses right and left. Used to be, he said, a doctor knew what he was treating, but he don't know any more.

I don't know if Bert or Amy told Doc about Heath, although I imagine that they didn't. After all, you don't tell a doctor that a neighbor cured your child. And there might have been someone who would have been ornery enough to try to bring a charge against Heath for practising medicine without a license, although that would have been pretty hard to prove. But the story got around the valley and there was a lot of talk. Heath, I heard, had been a famous doctor in Vienna before he'd made his getaway. But I didn't believe it. I don't even believe those who started the story believed it, but that's the way it goes in a neighborhood like ours.

That story, and others, made quite a flurry for a month or so, but then it quieted down and you could see that the Heaths had become one of us and belonged to the valley. Bert went over and had quite a talk with Heath and the womenfolks took to calling Mrs Heath on the telephone, with some of those who were listening in breaking in to say a word of two, thereby initiating Mrs Heath into the round-robin telephone conversations that are going on all the time on our valley party line, with it getting so that you have to bust in on them and tell them to get off the line when you want to make an important call. We had Heath out with us on our coon hunts that fall and some of the young bloods started paying attention to Heath's daughter. It was almost as if the Heaths were old-time residents.

As I've said before, we've always been real fortunate in getting in good neighbors.

When things are going well, time has a way of flowing along so smoothly that you aren't conscious of its passing, and that was the way it was in the valley.

We had good years, but none of us paid much attention to that. You don't pay much attention to the good times, you get so you take them for granted. It's only when bad times come along that you look back and realize the good times you have had.

A year or so ago I was just finishing up the morning chores when a car with a New York license pulled up at the barn-yard gate. It isn't very often we see an out-of-state license plate in the valley, so I figured that it probably was someone who had gotten lost and had stopped to ask directions. There was a man and woman in the front seat and three kids and a dog in the back seat and the car was new and shiny.

I was carrying the milk up from the barn and when the man got out I put the pails down on the ground and waited for him.

He was a youngish sort of fellow and he looked intelligent and he had good manners.

He told me his name was Rickard and that he was a New York newspaperman on vacation and had dropped into the valley on his way out west to check some information.

It was the first time, so far as I knew, that the valley had
28

ever been of any interest newswise and I said so. I said we never did much here to get into the news.

'It's no scandal,' Rickard told me, 'if that is what you're thinking. It's just a matter of statistics.'

There are a lot of times when I don't catch a situation as quickly as I should, being a sort of deliberate type, but it seems to me now that as soon as he said statistics I could see it coming.

'I did a series of farm articles a few months back,' said Rickard, 'and to get my information I had to go through a lot of government statistics. I never got so sick of anything in my entire life.'

'And?' I asked, not feeling too well myself.

'I found some interesting things about this valley,' he went on. 'I remember that I didn't catch it for a while. Went on past the figures for a ways. Almost missed the significance, in fact. Then I did a double-take and backed up and looked at them again. The full story wasn't in that report, of course. Just a hint of something. So I did some more digging and came up with other facts.'

I tried to laugh it off, but he wouldn't let me.

'Your weather, for one thing,' he said. 'Do you realize you've had perfect weather for the past ten years?'

'The weather's been pretty good,' I admitted.

'It wasn't always good. I went back to see.'

'That's right,' I said. 'It's been better lately.'

'Your crops have been the best they've ever been in the last ten years.'

'Better seed,' I said. 'Better ways of farming.'

He grinned at me. 'You guys haven't changed your way of farming in the last quarter century.'

And he had me there, of course.

'There was an army worm invasion two years ago,' he said. 'It hit all around you, but you got by scot-free.'

'We were lucky. I remember we said so at the time.'

'I checked the health records,' he said. 'Same thing once again. For ten solid years. No measles, no chicken-pox, no pneumonia. No nothing. One death in ten full years — complications attendant on old age.'

'Old Man Parks,' I said. 'He was going onto ninety. Fine old gentleman.'

'You see,' said Rickard.

I did see.

The fellow had the figures. He had tracked it down, this thing we hadn't even realized, and he had us cold.

'What do you want me to do about it?' I asked.

'I want to talk to you about a neighbor.'

'I won't talk about any of my neighbors. Why don't you talk to him yourself?'

'I tried to, but he wasn't at home. Fellow down the road said he'd gone to town. Whole family had gone into town.'

'Reginald Heath,' I said. There wasn't much sense in playing dumb with Rickard, for he knew all the angles.

'That's the man. I talked to folks in town. Found out he'd never had to have any repair work done on any of his machinery or his car. Has the same machinery he had when he started farming. And it was worn out then.'

'He takes good care of it,' I told him. 'He keeps it tinkered up.'

'Another thing,' said Rickard. 'Since he's been here he hasn't bought a drop of gasoline.'

I'd known the rest of it, of course, although I'd never stopped to think about it. But I didn't know about the gasoline. I must have shown my surprise, for Rickard grinned at me.

'What do you want?' I asked.

'A story.'

'Heath's the man to talk to. I don't know a thing to help you.'

And even when I said it I felt easy in my mind. I seemed to have an instinctive faith that Heath could handle the situation, that he'd know just what to do.

But after breakfast I couldn't settle down to work. I was pruning the orchard, a job I'd been putting off for a year or two and that badly needed doing. I kept thinking of that business of Heath not buying gasoline and that night I'd found the tractor plowing by itself and how smooth

30

both the car and tractor ran despite all the noise they made.

So I laid down my pruning hook and shears and struck out across the fields. I knew the Heath family was in town, but I don't think it would have made any difference to me if they'd been at home. I think I would have gone just the same. For more than ten years now, I realized, I'd been wondering about that tractor and it was time that I found out.

I found the tractor in the machine shed and I thought maybe I'd have some trouble getting into it. But I didn't have a bit. I slipped the catches and the hood lifted up and I found exactly what I had thought I'd find, except that I hadn't actually worked out in my mind the picture of what I'd find underneath that hood.

It was just a block of some sort of shining metal that looked almost like a cube of heavy glass. It wasn't very big, but it had a massive look about it, as if it might have been a heavy thing to lift.

You could see the old bolt holes where the original internal combustion engine had been mounted and a heavy piece of some sort of metal had been fused across the frame to seat that little power plant. And up above the shiny cube was an apparatus of some sort. I didn't take the time to find out how it worked, but I could see that it was connected to the exhaust and knew it was a dingus that disguised the power plant. You know how in electric trains they have it fixed up so that the locomotive goes *chuff-chuff* and throws out a stream of smoke. Well, that was what that contraption was. It threw out little puffs of smoke and made a tractor noise.

I stood there looking at it and I wondered why it was, if Heath had an engine that worked better than an internal combustion engine, he should have gone to so much trouble to hide the fact he had it. If I'd had a thing like that, I knew I'd make the most of it. I'd get someone to back me and go into production and in no time at all I'd be stinking rich. And there'd be nothing in the world to prevent Heath from doing that. But instead he'd fixed the

31

tractor so it looked and sounded like an ordinary tractor and he'd fixed his car to make so much noise that it hid the fact it had a new type motor. Only he had overdone it. He'd made both the car and tractor make more noise than they should. And he'd missed an important bet in not buying gasoline. In his place I'd bought the stuff, just the way you should, and thrown it away or burned it to get rid of it.

It almost seemed to me that Heath might have had something he was hiding all these years, that he'd tried deliberately to keep himself unnoticed. As if he might really have been a refugee from the Iron Curtain – or from somewhere else.

I put the hood back in place again and snapped the catches shut and when I went out I was very careful to shut the machine shed door securely.

I went back to my pruning and I did quite a bit of thinking and while I was doing it I realized that I'd been doing this same thinking, piecemeal, ever since that night I'd found the tractor running by itself. Thinking of it in snatches and not trying to correlate all my thinking and that way it hadn't added up to much, but now it did and I suppose I should have been a little scared.

But I wasn't scared. Reginald Heath was a neighbor, and a good one, and we'd gone hunting and fishing together and we'd helped one another with haying and threshing and one thing and another and I liked the man as well as anyone I had ever known. Sure, he was a little different and he had a funny kind of tractor and a funny kind of car and he might even have a way of stretching time and since he'd come into the valley we'd been fortunate in weather and in health. All true, of course, but nothing to be scared of. Nothing to be scared of, once you knew the man.

For some reason or other I remembered the time several years before when I'd dropped by of a summer evening. It was hot and the Heath family had brought chairs out on the lawn because it was cooler there. Heath got me a chair and we sat and talked, not about anything in particular, but whatever came into our heads.

There was no moon, but there were lots of stars and they were the prettiest I have ever seen them.

I called Heath's attention to them and, just shooting off my mouth, I told him what little I'd picked up about astronomy.

'They're a long ways off,' I said. 'So far off that their light takes years to reach us. And all of them are suns. A lot of them bigger than our sun.'

Which was about all I knew about the stars.

Heath nodded gravely.

'There's one up there,' he said, 'that I watch a lot. That blue one, over there. Well, sort of blue, anyhow. See it? See how it twinkles. Like it might be winking at us. A friendly sort of star.'

I pretended that I saw the one he was pointing at, although I wasn't sure I did, there were so many of them and a lot of them were twinkling.

Then we got to talking about something else and forgot about the stars. Or at least I did.

Right after supper, Bert Smith came over and said that Rickard had been around asking him some questions and that he'd been down to Jingo's place and that he'd said he'd see Heath just as soon as Heath got back from town.

Bert was a bit upset about it, so I tried to calm him down.

'These city folks get excited easy,' I told him. 'There's nothing to it.'

I didn't worry much about it because I felt sure that Heath could handle things and even if Rickard did write a story for the New York papers it wouldn't bother us. Coon Valley is a long piece from New York.

I figured we'd probably seen and heard the last from Rickard.

But in all my life, I've never been more wrong.

About midnight or so I woke up with Helen shaking me.

'There's someone at the door,' she said. 'Go see who it is.'

33

So I shucked into my overalls and shoes and lit the lamp and went downstairs to see.

While I'd been getting dressed there'd been some knocking at the door, but as soon as I lit the lamp it quit.

I went to the door and opened it and there stood Rickard and he wasn't near as chipper as he'd been in the morning.

'Sorry to get you up,' he said, 'but it seems that I'm lost.'

'You can't be lost,' I told him. 'There isn't but one road through the valley. One end of it ties up to Sixty and the other to Eighty-five. You follow the valley road and you're bound to hit one or the other of them.'

'I've been driving,' he told me, 'for the last four hours and I can't find either of them.'

'Look,' I said, 'all you do is drive one way or the other. You can't get off the road. Fifteen minutes either way and you're on the state highway.'

I was exasperated with him, for it seemed a silly thing to do. And I don't take kindly to being routed out at midnight.

'But I tell you I'm lost,' he said in a sort of desperation and I could see that he was close to panic. 'The wife is getting scared and the kids are dead on their feet – '

'All right,' I told him. 'Let me get on my shirt and tie my shoes. I'll get you out of here.'

He told me he wanted to get to Sixty, so I got out my car and told him to follow me. I was pretty sore about it, but I figured the only thing to do was to help him out. He'd upset the valley and the sooner out the better.

I drove for thirty minutes before I began to get confused myself. That was twice as long as it should have taken to get out to the highway. But the road looked all right and there seemed to be nothing wrong, except for the time it took. So I kept on going. At the end of forty-five minutes we were back in front of my place again.

I couldn't figure it out for the life of me. I got out of my car and went back to Rickard's car.

'You see what I mean,' he said.

'We must have got turned around,' I said.

His wife was almost hysterical.

'What's going on?' she asked me in a high, shrill voice. 'What is going on around here?'

'We'll try again,' I said. 'We'll drive slower this time so we don't make the same mistake.'

I drove slower and this time it took an hour to get back to the farm. So we tried for Eighty-five and forty minutes later were right back where we started.

'I give up,' I told them. 'Get out and come in. We'll fix up some beds. You can spend the night and we'll get you out come light.'

I cooked up some coffee and found stuff to make sandwiches while Helen fixed up beds to take care of the five of them.

'The dog can sleep out here in the kitchen,' she said.

I got an apple box and quilt and fixed the dog a bed.

The dog was a nice little fellow, a wire-hair who was full of fun, and the Rickard kids were about as fine a bunch of kids as you'd find anywhere.

Mrs Rickard was all set to have hysterics, but Helen got her to drink some coffee and I wouldn't let them talk about not being able to get out.

'Come daylight,' I told them, 'and there'll be nothing to it.'

After breakfast they were considerably calmed down and seemed to have no doubt they could find Number Sixty. So they started out alone, but in an hour were back again. I took my car and started out ahead of them and I don't mind admitting I could feel bare feet walking up and down my spine.

I watched closely and all at once I realized that somehow we were headed back into the valley instead of heading out of it. So I stopped the car and we turned our cars around and headed back in the right direction. But in ten minutes we were turned around again. We tried again and this time we fairly crawled, trying to spot the place where we got turned around. But we could never spot it.

We went back to my place and I called up Bert and Jingo and asked them to come over.

Both of them tried to lead the Rickards out, one at a

time, then the two of them together, but they were no better at it than I was. Then I tried it alone, without the Rickards following me, and I had no trouble at all. I was out to highway Sixty and back in half an hour. So we thought maybe the jinx was broken and I tried to lead out the Rickard car, but it was no soap.

By mid-afternoon we knew the answer. Any of the natives could get out of the valley, but the Rickards couldn't.

Helen put Mrs Rickard to bed and fed her some sedative and I went over to see Heath.

He was glad to see me and he listened to me, but all the time I was talking to him I kept remembering how one time I had wondered if maybe he could stretch out time. When I had finished he was silent for a while, as if he might have been going over some decision just to be certain that it was right.

'It's a strange business, Calvin,' he said finally, 'and it doesn't seem right the Rickards should be trapped in this valley if they don't want to stay here.

'Yet, it's a fortunate thing for us, actually. Rickard was planning on writing a story about us, and if he'd written as he planned to, there'd been a lot of attention paid us. There would have been a crowd of people coming in — other newspapermen and government men and people from the universities and the idly curious. They'd have upset our lives and some of them would have offered us big sums of money for our farms, much more than they're worth, and all of it would spoil the valley for us. I don't know about you, but I like the valley as it is. It reminds me of . . . well, of another place.'

'Rickard still can telephone that story,' I told him, 'or he can mail it out. Just keeping Rickard here won't prevent that story being printed.'

'Somehow I think it will,' he said. 'I am fairly certain he won't telephone it or send it in the mails.'

I had come half prepared to go to bat for Rickard, but I thought over what Heath had pointed out to me and I didn't do it.

I saw that if there were some principle or power which kept the valley healthy and insured good weather and made living pleasant, why, then, the rest of the world would be hell-bent to use the same principle or power. It might have been selfish of me, but I felt fairly certain the principle or power couldn't be spread thin enough to cover all the world. And if anyone were to have it, I wanted it kept right here, where it rightfully belonged.

And there was another thing: If the world should learn there was such a power or principle and if we couldn't share it or refused to share it, then all the world would be sore at us and we'd live in the center of a puddle of hatred.

I went back home and had a talk with Rickard and I didn't try to hide anything from him. He was all set to go and have it out with Heath, but I advised against it. I pointed out that he didn't have a shred of proof and he'd only make himself look silly, for Heath would more than likely act as if he didn't know what he was getting at. After quite a tussle, he took my advice.

The Rickards stayed on at our place for several days and occasionally Rickard and I would make a trial run just to test the situation out, but there was no change.

Finally Bert and Jingo came over and we had a council of war with the Rickard family. By this time Mrs Rickard was taking it somewhat better and the Rickard kids were happy with the outdoor life and the Rickard dog was busily engaged in running all the valley rabbits down to skin and bones.

'There's the old Chandler place up at the head of the valley,' said Jingo. 'No one's been living there for quite a while, but it's in good shape. It could be fixed up so it was comfortable.'

'But I can't stay here,' protested Rickard. 'I can't settle down here.'

'Who said anything about settling down?' asked Bert. 'You just got to wait it out. Some day whatever is wrong will get straightened out and then you can get away.'

'But my job,' said Rickard.

Mrs Rickard spoke up then. You could see she didn't

like the situation any better than he did, but she had the queer, practical, everyday logic that a woman at times surprised a man by showing. She knew that they were stuck here in the valley and she was out to make the best of it.

'Remember that book you're always threatening to write?' she asked. 'Maybe this is it.'

That did it.

Rickard mooned around for a while, making up his mind, although it already was made up. Then he began talking about the peace in the valley – the peace and quietness and the lack of hurry – just the place to write a book.

The neighbors got together and fixed up the house on the old Chandler place and Rickard called his office and made some excuse and got a leave of absence and wrote a letter to his bank, transferring whatever funds he had. Then he settled down to write.

Apparently in his phone calls and his letter writing he never even hinted at the real reason for his staying – perhaps because it would have sounded downright silly – for there was no ruckus over his failure to go back.

The valley settled down to its normal life again and it felt good after all the uproar. The neighbors shopped for the Rickards and carried out from town all the groceries and other things they needed and once in a while Rickard took the car and had a try at finding the state highways.

But mostly he wrote and in about a year he sold this book of his. Probably you have read it: *You Could Hear the Silence*. Made him a hunk of money. But his New York publishers still are going slowly mad trying to understand why he steadfastly refuses to stir out of the valley. He has refused lecture tours, has declined dinners in his honor and turned down all the other glitter that goes with writing a best seller.

The book didn't change Rickard at all. By the time he sold it he was well liked in the valley and seemed to like everyone – except possibly Heath. He stayed rather cold to Heath. He used to do a lot of walking, to get exercise, he said, although I think that he thought up most of his book out on those walks. And he'd stop by and chew the fat when he was out on those walks and that way everyone got to know him. He used to talk a lot about when he could get out of the valley and all of us were beginning to feel sorry that a time would come when he would leave, for the Rickards had turned out to be good neighbors. There must be something about the valley that brings out the best there is in everyone. As I have said before, we have yet to get a bad neighbor and that is something most neighborhoods can't say.

One day I had stopped on my way from town to talk a while with Heath and as we stood talking, up the road came Rickard. You could see he wasn't going anywhere, but was just out for a walk.

He stopped and talked with us for a few minutes, then suddenly he said. 'You know, we've made up our minds that we would like to stay here.'

'Now, that is fine,' said Heath.

'Grace and I were talking about it the other night,' said Rickard. 'About the time when we could get out of here. Then suddenly we stopped our talking and looked at one another and we knew right then and there we didn't want to leave. It's been so peaceful and the kids like the school here so much better than in the city and the people are so fine we couldn't bear to leave.'

'I'm glad to hear you say that,' Heath told him. 'But it seems to me you've been sticking pretty close. You ought to take the wife and kids in town to see a show.'

And that was it. It was as simple as all that.

Life goes on in the valley as it always has, except it's even better now. All of us are healthy. We don't even seem to get colds any more. When we need rain we get it and when there's need for sun the sun is sure to shine. We aren't getting rich, for you can't get rich with all this Washington interference, but we're making a right good living. Rickard is working on his second book and once in a while I go out at night and try to locate the star Heath showed me that evening long ago.

But we still get some publicity now and then. The other night I was listening to my favorite newscaster and he had an item he had a lot of fun with.

'Is there really such a place as Coon Valley?' he asked and you could hear the chuckle just behind the words. 'If there is, the government would like to know about it. The maps insist there is and there are statistics on the books that say it's a place where there is no sickness, where the climate is ideal, where there's never a crop failure – a land of milk and honey. Investigators have gone out to seek the truth of this and they can't find the place, although people in nearby communities insist there's such a valley. Telephone calls have been made to people listed as residents of the valley, but the calls can't be completed. Letters have been written to them, but the letters are returned to the sender for one or another of the many reasons the post-office has for non-delivery. Investigators have waited in nearby trading centers, but Coon Valley people never came to town while the investigators were there. If there is such a place and if the things the statistics say of it are true, the government would be very interested, for there must be data in the valley that could be studied and applied to other sectors. We have no way of knowing whether this broadcast can reach the valley – if it is any more efficient than investigators or telephone or the post service. But if it does – and if there is such a place as Coon Valley – and if one of its residents should be listening, won't he please speak up!'

He chuckled then, chuckled very briefly, and went on to tell the latest rumor about Khrushchev.

I shut off the radio and sat in my chair and thought about the times when for several days no one could find his way out of the valley and of the other times when the telephones went dead for no apparent reason. And I remembered how we'd talked about it among ourselves and wondered if we should speak to Heath about it, but had in each case decided not to, since we felt that Heath knew what he was doing and that we could trust his judgment.

It's inconvenient at times, of course, but there are a lot of compensations. There hasn't been a magazine solicitor in the valley for more than a dozen years — nor an insurance salesman, either.

GREEN THUMB

I had come back from lunch and was watching the office while Millie went out to get a bite to eat. With my feet up on the desk in a comfortable position, I was giving considerable attention to how I might outwit a garbage-stealing dog.

The dog and I had carried on a feud for months and I was about ready to resort to some desperate measures.

I had blocked up the can with heavy concrete blocks so he couldn't tip it over, but he was a big dog and could stand up and reach down into the can and drag all the garbage out. I had tried putting a heavy weight on the lid, but he simply dragged it off and calmly proceeded with his foraging. I had waited up and caught him red-handed at it and heaved some rocks and whatever else was handy at him, but he recognized tactics such as these for what they were and they didn't bother him. He'd come back in half an hour, calm as ever.

I had considered setting a light muskrat trap on top of the garbage so that, when he reached down into the can, he'd get his muzzle caught. But if I did that, sure as hell I'd forget to take it out some Tuesday morning and the garbage-man would get caught instead. I had toyed with the idea of wiring the can so the dog would get an electric shock when he came fooling around. But I didn't know how to go about wiring it and, if I did, ten to one I'd fix it up so I'd electrocute him instead of just scaring him off, and I didn't want to kill him.

I like dogs, you understand. That doesn't mean I have to like *all* dogs, does it? And if you had to scrape up garbage every morning, you'd be just as sore at the mutt as I was.

While I was wondering if I couldn't put something in a particularly tempting bit of garbage that would make him sick and still not kill him, the phone rang.

It was old Pete Skinner out on Acorn Ridge.

'Could you come out?' he asked.

'Maybe,' I said. 'What you got?'

'I got a hole out in the north forty.'

'Sink-hole?'

'Nope. Looks like someone dug it out and carried off the dirt.'

'Who would do that, Pete?'

'I don't know. And that ain't all of it. They left a pile of sand beside the hole.'

'Maybe that's what they dug out of the hole.'

'You know well enough,' said Pete, 'that I haven't any sandy soil. You've run tests enough on it. All of mine is clay.'

'I'll be right out,' I told him.

A county agent gets some funny calls, but this one topped them all. Hog cholera, corn borers, fruit blight, milk production records – any of these would have been down my alley. But a hole in the north forty?

And yet, I suppose I should have taken it as a compliment that Pete called me. When you've been a county agent for fifteen years, a lot of farmers get to trust you and some of them, like Pete, figure you can straighten out any problem. I enjoy a compliment as much as anybody. It's the headaches that go with them that I don't like.

When Millie came back, I drove out to Pete's place, which is only four or five miles out of town.

Pete's wife told me that he was up in the north forty, so I went there and found not only Pete, but some of his

43

neighbors. All of them were looking at the hole and doing a lot of talking. I never saw a more puzzled bunch of people.

The hole was about thirty feet in diameter and about thirty-five feet deep, an almost perfect cone – not the kind of hole you'd dig with a pick and shovel. The sides were cut as clean as if they'd been machined, but the soil was not compressed, as it would have been if machinery had been used.

The pile of sand lay just a short distance from the hole. Looking at it, I had the insane feeling that, if you shovelled that sand into the hole, it would exactly fit. It was the whitest sand I've ever seen and, when I walked over to the pile and picked up some of it, I saw that it was clean. Not just ordinary clean, but *absolutely* clean – as though laundered grain by grain.

I stood around for a while, like the rest of them, staring at the hole and the pile of sand and wishing I could come up with some bright idea. But I wasn't able to. There was the hole and there was the sand. The topsoil was dry and powdery and would have shown wheelmarks or any other kind if there'd been any. There weren't.

I told Pete maybe he'd better fence in the whole business, because the sheriff or somebody from the state, or even the university, might want to look it over. Pete said that was a good idea and he'd do it right away.

I went back to the farmhouse and asked Mrs Skinner to give me a couple of fruit jars. One of them I filled with a sample from the sand pile and the other with soil from the hole, being careful not to jolt the walls.

By this time, Pete and a couple of the neighbors had gotten a wagon-load of fence posts and some wire and were coming out to the field. I waited and helped unload the posts and wire, then drove back to the office, envying Pete. He was satisfied to put up the fence and let me worry about the problem.

I found three fellows waiting for me. I gave Millie the fruit jars and asked her to send them right away to the Soils Bureau at the State Farm Campus. Then I settled down to work.

Other people drifted in and it was late in the afternoon before I could call up the Soils Bureau and tell them I wanted the contents of the two jars analysed. I told them a little of what had happened, although not all of it, for, when you tried to put it into words, it sounded pretty weird.

'Banker Stevens called and asked if you'd drop by his place on your way home,' Millie told me.

'What would Stevens want with me?' I asked. 'He isn't a farmer and I don't owe him any money.'

'He grows fancy flowers,' said Millie.

'I know that. He lives just up the street from me.'

'From what I gathered, something awful happened to them. He was all broken up.'

So, on the way home, I stopped at the Stevens place. The banker was out in the yard waiting for me. He looked terrible. He led me around to the big flower garden in the back and never have I seen such utter devastation. In that whole area, there wasn't a single plant alive. Every one of them had given up the ghost and was lying wilted on the ground.

'What could have done it, Joe?' asked Stevens and, the way he said it, I felt sorry for him.

After all, those flowers were a big thing in his life. He'd raised them from special seed and he'd babied them along, and for anybody who is crazy about flowers, I imagine they were tops.

'Someone might have used some spray on them,' I said. 'Almost any kind of spray, if you don't dilute it enough, would kill them.'

Out in the garden, I took a close look at the dead flowers, but nowhere could I see any sign of the burning from too strong a spray.

Then I saw the holes, at first only two or three of them, then, as I went on looking, dozens of them. They were all over the garden, about an inch in diameter, for all the world as if someone had taken a broomstick and punched holes all over the place. I got down on my knees and could

45

see that they tapered, the way they do when you pull weeds with big taproots out of the ground.

'You been pulling weeds?' I asked.

'Not big ones like that,' said the banker. 'I take good care of those flowers, Joe. You know that. Keep them weeded and watered and cultivated and sprayed. Put just the right amount of commercial fertilizer in the soil. Try to keep it at top fertility.'

'You should use manure. It's better than all the commercial fertilizer you can buy.'

'I don't agree with you. Tests have proved . . .'

It was an old argument, one that we fought out each year. I let him run on, only half listening to him, while I picked up some of the soil and crumbled it. It was dead soil. You could feel that it was. It crumbled at the lightest touch and was dry, even when I dug a foot beneath the surface.

'You water this bed recently?' I asked.

'Last evening,' Stevens said.

'When did you find the flowers like this?'

'This morning. They looked fine last night. And now . . .' he blinked fast.

I asked him for a fruit jar and filled it with a sample of the soil.

'I'll send this in and see if there's anything wrong with it,' I said.

A bunch of dogs were barking at something in the hedge in front of my place when I got home. Some of the dogs in the neighborhood are hell on cats. I parked the car and picked up an old hoe handle and went out to rescue the cat they seemed to have cornered.

They scattered when they saw me coming and I started to look in the hedge for the cat. There wasn't any and that aroused my curiosity and I wondered what the dogs could have been barking at. So I went hunting.

And I found it.

It was lying on the ground, close against the lower growth of the hedge, as if it had crawled there for protection.

I reached in and pulled it out — a weed of some sort, about five feet tall, and with a funny root system. There were eight roots, each about an inch in diameter at the top and tapering to a quarter-inch or so. They weren't all twisted up, but were sort of sprung out, so that there were four to the side, each set of four in line. I looked at their tips and I saw that the roots were not broken off, but ended in blunt, strong points.

The stalk, at the bottom, was about as thick as a man's fist. There were four main branches covered with thick, substantial, rather meaty leaves; but the last foot of the branches was bare of leaves. At the top were several flower or seed pouches, the biggest of them the size of an old-fashioned coffee mug.

I squatted there looking at it. The more I looked, the more puzzled I became. As a county agent, you have to know quite a bit about botany and this plant was like none I had seen before.

I dragged it across the lawn to the tool-shed back of the garage and tossed it in there, figuring that after supper I'd have a closer look at it.

I went in the house to get my evening meal ready and decided to broil a steak and fix up a bowl of salad.

A lot of people in town wonder at my living in the old homestead, but I'm used to the house and there seemed to be no sense in moving somewhere else when all it costs me is taxes and a little upkeep. For several years before Mother died, she had been quite feeble and I did all the cleaning and helped with the cooking, so I'm fairly handy at it.

After I washed the dishes, I read what little there was to read in the evening paper and then looked up an old text on botany, to see if I could find anything that might help identify the plant.

I didn't find anything and, just before I went to bed, I got a flashlight and went out, imagining, I suppose, that I'd find the weed somehow different from the way I remembered it.

I opened the door of the shed and flashed the light

where I'd tossed the weed on the floor. At first I couldn't see it, then I heard a leafy rustling over in one corner and I turned the light in that direction.

The weed had crawled over to one corner and it was trying to get up, its stem bowed out – the way a man would arch his back – pressing against the wall of the shed.

Standing there with my mouth open, watching it try to raise itself erect, I felt horror and fear. I reached out to the corner nearest the door and snatched up an axe.

If the plant had succeeded in getting up, I might have chopped it to bits. But, as I stood there, I saw the thing would never make it. I was not surprised when it slumped back on the floor.

What I did next was just as unreasoning and instinctive as reaching for the axe.

I found an old washtub and half filled it with water. Then I picked up the plant – it had a squirmish feel to it, like a worm – stuck its roots into the water, and pushed the tub back against the wall, so the thing could be braced upright.

I went into the house and ransacked a couple of closets until I found the sunlamp I'd bought a couple of years back, to use when I had a touch of arthritis in my shoulder. I rigged up the lamp and trained it on the plant, not too close. Then I got a big shovelful of dirt and dumped it in the tub.

And that, I figured, was about all I could do. I was giving the plant water, soil-food and simulated sunlight. I was afraid that, if I tried a more fancy treatment, I might kill it, for I hadn't any notion of what conditions it might be used to.

Apparently I handled it right. It perked up considerably and, as I moved about, the coffee-cup-sized pod on the top kept turning, following every move I made.

I watched it for a while and moved the sunlamp back a little, so there'd be no chance of scorching it, and went back into the house.

It was then that I really began to get bone-scared. I had

been frightened out in the shed, of course, but that had been shock. Now, thinking it over, I began to understand more clearly what sort of creature I'd found underneath the hedge. I remember I wasn't yet ready to say it out loud, but it seemed probable that my guest was an alien intelligence.

I did some wondering about how it had gotten here and if it had made the holes in Banker Stevens' flowerbed and also if it could have had anything to do with the big hole out in Pete Skinner's north forty.

I sat around, arguing with myself, for a man just does not go prowling around in his neighbor's garden after midnight.

But I had to know.

I walked up the alley to the back of the Stevens house and sneaked into the garden. Shielding the flashlight with my hat, I had another look at the holes in the ruined flowerbed. I wasn't too surprised when I saw that they occurred in series of eight, four to the side – exactly the kind of holes the plant back in my tool-shed would make if it sank its roots into the ground.

I counted at least eleven of those eight-in-line sets of holes and I'm sure that there were more. But I didn't want to stick around too long, for fear Banker Stevens might wake up and ask questions.

So I went back home, down the alley, and was just in time to catch that garbage-stealing dog doing a good job on the can. He had his head stuck clear down into it and I was able to sneak up behind him. He heard me and struggled to get out, but he'd jammed himself into the can. Before he could get loose, I landed a good swift kick where it did maximum good. He set some kind of canine speed record in getting off the premises, I imagine.

I went to the tool-shed and opened the door. The tub half full of muddy water was still there and the sunlamp was still burning – but the plant was gone. I looked all over the shed and couldn't find it. So I unplugged the sunlamp and headed for the house.

To be truthful, I was a little relieved that the plant had wandered off.

But when I rounded the corner of the house, I saw it hadn't. It was in the window box, and the geraniums I had nursed all spring were hanging limply over the side of the box.

I stood there and looked at it and had the feeling that it was looking back at me.

And I remembered that not only had it had to travel from the tool-shed to the house and then climb into the window box, but it had had to open the tool-shed door and close it again.

It was standing up, stiff and straight, and appeared to be in the best of health. It looked thoroughly incongruous in the window box – as if a man had grown a tall stalk of corn there, although it didn't look anything like a stalk of corn.

I got a pail of water and poured it into the window box. Then I felt something tapping me on the head and looked up. The plant had bent over and was patting me with one of its branches. The modified leaf at the end of the branch had spread itself out to do the patting and looked something like a hand.

I went into the house and up to bed and the main thing I was thinking about was that, if the plant got too troublesome or dangerous, all I had to do was mix a strong dose of commercial fertilizer or arsenic, or something just as deadly, and water it with the mixture.

Believe it or not, I went to sleep.

Next morning I got to thinking that maybe I should repair the old greenhouse and put my guest in there and be sure to keep the door locked. It seemed to be reasonably friendly and inoffensive, but I couldn't be sure, of course.

After breakfast, I went out into the yard to look for it, with the idea of locking it in the garage for the day, but it wasn't in the window box, or anywhere that I could see. And since it was Saturday, when a lot of farmers came to town, with some of them sure to be dropping in to see me, I didn't want to be late to work.

I was fairly busy during the day and didn't have much time for thinking or worrying. But when I was wrapping up the sample of soil from the banker's garden to send to the Soils Bureau, I wondered if maybe there wasn't someone at the university I should notify. I also wondered about letting someone in Washington know, except I didn't have the least idea whom to contact, or even which department.

Coming home that evening, I found the plant anchored in the garden, in a little space where the radishes and lettuce had been. The few lettuce plants still left in the ground were looking sort of limp, but everything else was all right. I took a good look at the plant. It waved a couple of its branches at me – and it wasn't the wind blowing them, for there wasn't any wind – and it nodded its coffee-cup pod as if to let me know it recognized me. But that was all it did.

After supper, I scouted the hedge in front of the house and found two more of the plants. Both of them were dead.

My next-door neighbors had gone to a movie, so I scouted their place, too, and found four more of the plants, under bushes and in corners where they had crawled away to die.

I wondered whether it might not have been the plant I'd rescued that the dogs had been barking at the night before. I felt fairly sure it was. A dog might be able to recognize an alien being where a man would be unable to.

I counted up. At least seven of the things had picked out Banker Stevens' flowerbed for a meal and the chemical fertilizer he used had killed all but one of them. The sole survivor, then, was out in the garden, killing off my lettuce.

I wondered why the lettuce and geraniums and Stevens' flowers had reacted as they did. It might be that the alien plants produced some sort of poison, which they injected into the soil to discourage other plant life from crowding their feeding grounds. That was not exactly far-fetched. There are trees and plants on Earth that accomplish the

51

same thing by various methods. Or it might be that the aliens sucked the soil so dry of moisture and plant food that the other plants simply starved to death.

I did some wondering on why they'd come to Earth at all and why some of them had stayed. If they had travelled from some other planet, they must have come in a ship, so that hole out in Pete's north forty might have been where they stopped to replenish their food supply, dumping the equivalent of garbage beside the hole.

And what about the seven I had counted?

Could they have jumped ship? Or gone on shore leave and run into trouble, the way human sailors often do?

Maybe the ship had searched for the missing members of the party, had been unable to find them, and had gone on. If that were so, then my own plant was a marooned alien. Or maybe the ship was still hunting.

I wore myself out, thinking about it, and went to bed early, but lay there tossing for a long time. Then, just as I was falling asleep, I heard the dog at the garbage can. You'd think after what had happened to him the night before, that he'd have decided to skip that particular can, but not him. He was rattling and banging it around, trying to tip it over.

I picked a skillet off the stove and opened the back door. I got a good shot at him, but missed him by a good ten feet. I was so sore that I didn't even go out to pick up the skillet, but went back to bed.

It must have been several hours later that I was brought straight up in bed by the terror-stricken yelping of a dog. I jumped out and ran to the window. It was a bright moonlit night and the dog was going down the driveway as if the devil himself were after him. Behind him sailed the plant. It had wrapped one of its branches around his tail and the other three branches were really giving him a working over.

They went up the street out of sight and, for a long time after they disappeared, I could hear the dog still yelping. Within a few minutes, I saw the plant coming up the gravel, walking like a spider on its eight roots.

It turned off the driveway and planted itself beside a lilac bush and seemed to settle down for the night. I decided that if it wasn't good for anything else, the garbage can would be safe, at least. If the dog came back again, the plant would be waiting to put the bee on him.

I lay awake for a long time, wondering how the plant had known I didn't want the dog raiding the garbage. It probably had seen — if that is the proper word — me chase him out of the yard.

I went to sleep with the comfortable feeling that the plant and I had finally begun to understand each other.

The next day was Sunday and I started working on the greenhouse, putting it into shape so I could cage up the plant. It had found itself a sunny spot in the garden and was imitating a large and particularly ugly weed I'd been too lazy to pull out.

My next-door neighbor came over to offer free advice, but he kept shifting uneasily and I knew there was something on his mind.

Finally he came out with it. 'Funny thing — Jenny swears she saw a big plant walking around in your yard the other day. The kid saw it, too, and he claims it chased him.' He tittered a little, embarrassed. 'You know how kids are.'

'Sure,' I said.

He stood around a while longer and gave me some more advice, then went across the yard and home.

I worried about what he had told me. If the plant really had taken to chasing kids, there'd be hell to pay.

I worked at the greenhouse all day long, but there was a lot to do, for it had been out of use ten years or more, and by nightfall I was tuckered out.

After supper, I went out on the back stoop and sat on the steps, watching the stars. It was quiet and restful.

I hadn't been there more than fifteen minutes when I heard a rustling. I looked around and there was the plant, coming up out of the garden, walking along on its roots.

It sort of squatted down beside me and the two of us just sat there, looking at the stars. Or, at least, I looked at

53

them. I don't actually know if the plant could see. If it couldn't, it had some other faculty that was just as good as sight. We just sat there.

After a while, the plant moved one of its branches over and took hold of my arm with that handlike leaf. I tensed a bit, but its touch was gentle enough and I sat still, figuring that if the two of us were to get along, we couldn't start out by flinching away from one another.

Then, so gradually that at first I didn't notice it, I began to perceive a sense of gratitude, as if the plant might be thanking me. I looked around to see what it was doing and it wasn't doing a thing, just sitting there as I was, but with its 'hand' still on my arm.

Yet in some way, the plant was trying to make me understand that it was grateful to me for saving it.

It formed no words, you understand. Other than rustling its leaves, it couldn't make a sound. But I understood that some system of communication was in operation. No words, but emotion – deep, clear, utterly sincere emotion.

It eventually got a little embarrassing, this nonstop gratitude.

'Oh, that's all right,' I said, trying to put an end to it. 'You would have done as much for me.'

Somehow, the plant must have sensed that its thanks had been accepted, because the gratitude wore off a bit and something else took over – a sense of peace and quiet.

The plant got up and started to walk off and I called out to it, 'Hey, Plant, wait a minute!'

It seemed to understand that I had called it back, for it turned around. I took it by a branch and started to lead it around the boundaries of the yard. If this communication business was going to be any good, you see, it had to go beyond the sense of gratitude and peace and quiet. So I led the plant all the way around the yard and I kept thinking at it as hard as I could, telling it not to go beyond that perimeter.

By the time I'd finished, I was wringing wet with effort. But, finally, the plant seemed to be trying to say okay. Then I built up a mental image of it chasing a kid and I shook a mental finger at it. The plant agreed. I tried to tell it not to move around the yard in daylight, when people would be able to see it. Whether the concept was harder or I was getting tired, I don't know, but both the plant and I were limp when it at last indicated that it understood.

Lying in bed that night, I thought a lot about this problem of communication. It was not telepathy, apparently, but something based on mental pictures and emotions.

But I saw it as my one chance. If I could learn to converse, no matter how, and the plant could learn to communicate something beyond abstracts to me, it could talk to people, would be acceptable and believable, and the authorities might be willing to recognize it as an intelligent being. I decided that the best thing to do would be to acquaint it with the way we humans lived and try to make it understand why we lived that way. And since I couldn't take my visitor outside the yard, I'd have to do it inside.

I went to sleep, chuckling at the idea of my house and yard being a classroom for an alien.

The next day I received a phone call from the Soils Bureau at the university.

'What kind of stuff is this you're sending us?' the man demanded.

'Just some soil I picked up,' I said. 'What's wrong with it?'

'Sample One is all right. It's just common, everyday Burton County soil. But Sample Two, that sand – good God, man, it has gold dust and flakes of silver and some copper in it! All of it in minute particles, of course. But if some farmer out your way has a pit of that stuff, he's rich.'

'At the most, he has twenty-five or thirty truckloads of it.'

'Where'd he get it? Where'd it come from?'

I took a deep breath and told him all I knew about the incident out at Pete's north forty.

He said he'd be right out, but I caught him before he hung up and asked him about the third sample.

'What was he growing on that ground?' the man asked baffledly. 'Nothing I know of could suck it that clean, right down to the bare bone! Tell him to put in a lot of organic material and some lime and almost everything else that's needed in good soil, before he tries to use it.'

The soils people came out to Pete's place and they brought along some other men from the university. A little later in the week, after the papers had spelled out big headlines, a couple of men from Washington showed up. But no one seemed able to figure it out and they finally gave up. The newspapers gave it a play and dropped it as soon as the experts did.

During that time, curiosity seekers flocked to the farm to gape at the hole and the pile of sand. They had carried off more than half the sand and Pete was madder than hell about the whole business.

'I'm going to fill in that hole and forget all about it,' he told me, and that was what he did.

Meanwhile, at home, the situation was progressing. Plant seemed to understand what I had told him about not moving out of the yard and acting like a weed during the daytime and leaving kids alone. Everything was peaceable and I got no more complaints. Best of all, the garbage-stealing dog never showed his snout again.

Several times, during all the excitement out at Pete's place, I had been tempted to tell someone from the university about Plant. In each case, I decided not to, for we weren't getting along too well in the talk department.

But in other ways we were doing just fine.

I let Plant watch me while I took an electric motor apart and then put it together again, but I wasn't too sure he knew what it was all about. I tried to show him the concept of mechanical power and I demonstrated how the motor would deliver that power and I tried to tell him what electricity was. But I got all bogged down with that, not knowing too much about it myself. I don't honestly think Plant got a thing out of that electric motor.

With the motor of the car, though, we were more successful. We spent one whole Sunday dismantling it and then putting it back together. Watching what I was doing, Plant seemed to take a lot of interest in it.

We had to keep the garage door locked and it was a scorcher of a day and, anyhow, I'd much rather spend a Sunday fishing than tearing down a motor. I wondered a dozen times if it was worth it, if there might not be easier ways to teach Plant the facts of our Earth culture.

I was all tired out and failed to hear the alarm and woke up an hour later than I should. I jumped into my clothes, ran out to the garage, unlocked the door and there was Plant. He had parts from that motor strewn all over the floor and he was working away at it, happy as a clam. I almost took an axe to him, but I got hold of myself in time. I locked the door behind me and walked to work.

All day, I wondered how Plant had gotten into the garage. Had he sneaked back in the night before, when I wasn't looking, or had he been able to pick the lock? I wondered, too, what sort of shape I'd find the car in when I got home. I could just see myself working half the night, putting it back together.

I left work a little early. If I had to work on the car, I wanted an early start.

When I got home, the motor was all assembled and Plant was out in the garden, acting like a weed. Seeing him there, I realized he knew how to unlock the door, for I'd locked it when I left that morning.

I turned on the ignition, making bets with myself that it wouldn't start. But it did. I rode around town a little to check it and there wasn't a thing wrong with it.

For the next lesson, I tried something simpler. I got my carpentry tools and showed them to Plant and let him watch me while I made a bird house. Not that I needed any more bird houses. The place already crawled with them. But it was the easiest, quickest thing I could think of to show Plant how we worked in wood.

He watched closely and seemed to understand what was going on, all right, but I detected a sadness in him. I put my hand on his arm to ask him what was the matter.

All that I got was a mournful reaction.

It bewildered me. Why should Plant take so much interest in monkeying around with a motor and then grieve at the making of a bird house? I didn't get it figured out until a few days later, when Plant saw me picking a bouquet of flowers for the kitchen table.

And then it hit me.

Plant was a plant and flowers were plants and so was lumber, or at least lumber at one time had been a plant. And I stood there, with the bouquet dangling in my hand and Plant looking at me, and I thought of all the shocks we had in store for him when he found out more about us – how we slaughtered our forests, grew plants for food and clothing, squeezed or boiled drugs from them.

It was just like a human going to another planet, I realized, and finding that some alien life form grew humans for food.

Plant didn't seem to be sore at me nor did he shrink from me in horror. He was just sad. When he got sad, he was the saddest-looking thing you could possibly imagine. A bloodhound with a hangover would have looked positively joyous in comparison.

If we ever had gotten to the point where we could have really talked – about things like ethics and philosophy, I mean – I might have learned just how Plant felt about our plant-utilizing culture. I'm sure he tried to tell me, but I couldn't understand much of what he was driving at.

We were sitting out on the steps one night, looking at the stars. Earlier, Plant had been showing me his home planet, or it may have been some of the planets he had visited. I don't know. All I could get were fuzzy mental pictures and reactions. One place was hot and red, another blue and cold. There was another that had all the colours of the rainbow and a cool, restful feel about it, as if there might have been gentle winds and fountains and birdsongs in the twilight.

We had been sitting there for quite a while when he put his hand back on my arm again and he showed me a plant. He must have put considerable effort into getting me to visualize it, for the image was sharp and clear. It

58

was a scraggy, run-down plant and it looked even sadder than Plant looked when he got sad, if that is possible. When I started feeling sorry for it, he began to think of kindness and, when he thought of things like kindness and sadness and gratitude and happiness, he could really pour it on.

He had me thinking such big, kindly thoughts, I was afraid that I would burst. While I sat there, thinking that way, I saw the plant begin to perk up. It grew and flowered and was the most beautiful thing I had ever seen. It matured its seeds and dropped them. Swiftly, little plants sprang from the seeds and they were healthy and full of ginger, too.

I mulled that one over several days, suspecting I was crazy for even thinking what I did. I tried to shrug it off, but it wouldn't shrug. It gave me an idea.

The only way I could get rid of it was to try it out.

Out in back of the tool-shed was the sorriest yellow rose in town. Why it clung to life, year after year, I could never figure out. It had been there ever since I was a boy. The only reason it hadn't been dug up and thrown away long ago was that no one had ever needed the ground it was rooted in.

I thought, if a plant ever needed help, that yellow rose was it.

So I sneaked out back of the tool-shed, making sure that Plant didn't see me, and stood in front of that yellow rose. I began to think kindly thoughts about it, although God knows it was hard to think kindly toward such a wretched thing. I felt foolish and hoped none of the neighbors spotted me, but I kept at it. I didn't seem to accomplish much to start with, but I went back, time after time. In a week or so, I got so that I just naturally loved that yellow rose to pieces.

After four or five days, I began to see some change in it. At the end of two weeks, it had developed from a scraggy, no-account bush to one that any rose fancier would have been proud to own. It dropped its bug-chewed leaves and grew new ones that were so shiny they looked as if they were waxed. Then it grew big flower buds and, in no time at all, was a blaze of yellow glory.

But I didn't quite believe it. In the back of my mind, I figured that Plant must have seen me doing it and helped along a bit. So I decided to test the process again where he couldn't interfere.

Millie had been trying for a couple of years to grow an African violet in a flower pot at the office. By this time, even she was willing to admit it was a losing battle. I had made a lot of jokes about the violet and, at times, Millie had been sore at me about it. Like the yellow rose, it was a hard-luck plant. The bugs ate it. Millie forgot to water it. It got knocked onto the floor. Visitors used it for an ashtray.

Naturally, I couldn't give it the close, intensive treatment I'd given the rose, but I made a point to stop for a few minutes every day beside the violet and think good things about it and, in a couple of weeks, it perked up considerably. By the end of the month, it had bloomed for the first time in its life.

Meanwhile, Plant's education continued.

At first, he'd balked at entering the house, but finally trusted me enough to go in. He didn't spend much time there, for the house was too full of reminders that ours was a plant-utilizing culture. Furniture, clothing, cereal, paper – even the house itself – all were made of vegetation. I got an old butter tub and filled it with soil and put it in one corner of the dining-room, so he could eat in the house if he wanted to, but I don't remember that he even once took a snack out of that tub.

Although I didn't admit it then, I knew that what Plant and I had tried to do had been a failure. Whether someone else might have done better, I don't know. I suspect he might have. But I didn't know how to go about getting in touch and I was afraid of being laughed at. It's a terrible thing, our human fear of ridicule.

And there was Plant to consider, too. How would he take being passed on to someone else? I'd screw up my courage to do something about it, and then Plant would come up out of the garden and sit beside me on the steps, and we'd talk – not about anything that mattered, really, but about happiness and sadness and brotherhood, and my courage would go glimmering and I'd have to start all over again.

I've since thought how much like two lost children we must have been, strange kids raised in different countries, who would have liked to play together, except neither knew the rules for the other's games or spoke the other's language.

I know . . . I know. According to common sense, you begin with mathematics. You show the alien that you know two and two are four. Then you draw the solar system and show him the sun on the diagram and then point to the sun overhead and you point to Earth on the diagram, then point to yourself. In this way, you demonstrate to him that you know about the solar system and about space and the stars and so on.

Then you hand him the paper and the pencil.

But what if he doesn't know mathematics? What if the two-plus-two-makes-four routine doesn't mean a thing to him? What if he's never seen a drawing? What if he can't draw – or see or hear or feel or think the way you do?

To deal with an alien, you've got to get down to basics.

And maybe maths isn't basic.

Maybe diagrams aren't.

In that case, you have to search for something that is.

Yet there must be certain universal basics.

I think I know what they are.

That, if nothing else, Plant taught me.

Happiness is basic. And sadness is basic. And gratitude, in perhaps a lesser sense. Kindness, too. And perhaps hatred – although Plant and I never dealt in that.

Maybe brotherhood. For the sake of humanity, I hope so.

But kindness and happiness and brotherhood are awkward tools to use in reaching specific understanding, although in Plant's world they may not be.

It was getting on toward autumn and I was beginning to

wonder how I'd take care of Plant during the winter months.

I could have kept him in the house, but he hated it there.

Then, one night, we were sitting on the back steps, listening to the first crickets of the season.

The ship came down without a sound. I didn't see it until it was about at treetop level. It floated down and landed between the house and tool-shed.

I was startled for a moment, but not frightened, and perhaps not too surprised. In the back of my head, I'd wondered all the time, without actually knowing it, whether Plant's pals might not ultimately find him.

The ship was a shimmery sort of thing, as if it might not have been made of metal and was not really solid. I noticed that it had not really landed, but floated a foot or so above the grass.

Three other Plants stepped out and the oddest part of it was that there wasn't any door. They just came out of the ship and the ship closed behind them.

Plant took me by the arm and twitched it just a little, to make me understand he wanted me to walk with him to the ship. He made little comforting thoughts to try to calm me down.

And all the time that this was going on, I could sense the talk between Plant and those other three — but just grasping the fringe of the conversation, barely knowing there was talk, not aware of what was being said.

And then, while Plant stood beside me, with his hand still on my arm, those other plants walked up. One by one, each took me by the other arm and stood facing me for a moment and told me thanks and happiness.

Plant told me the same, for the last time, and then the four of them walked toward the ship and disappeared into it. The ship left me standing there, watching it rise into the night, until I couldn't see it any longer.

I stood there for a long time, staring up into the sky, with the thanks and happiness fading and loneliness beginning to creep in.

I knew that, somewhere up there, was a larger ship, that in it were many other Plants, that one of them had lived with me for almost six months and that others of them had died in the hedges and fence corners of the neighborhood. I knew also that it had been the big ship that had scooped out the load of nutritious soil from Pete Skinner's field.

Finally I stopped looking at the sky. Over behind the tool-shed I saw the whiteness of the yellow rose in bloom and once again I thought about the basics.

I wondered if happiness and kindness, perhaps even emotions that we humans do not know, might not be used on Plant's world as we use the sciences.

For the rose bush had bloomed when I thought kindly thoughts of it. And the African violet had found a new life in the kindness of a human.

Startling as it may seem, foolish as it may sound, it is not an unknown phenomenon. There are people who have the knack of getting the most out of a flowerbed or a garden. And it is said of these people that they have green thumbs.

May it not be that *green thumbness* is not so much concerned with skill or how much care is taken of a plant, as with the kindliness and the interest of the person tending it?

For aeons, the plant life of this planet has been taken for granted. It is simply there. By and large, plants are given little affection. They are planted or sown. They grow. In proper season, they are harvested.

I sometimes wonder if, as hunger tightens its grip upon our teeming planet, there may not be a vital need for the secret of *green thumbness*.

If kindness and sympathy can cause a plant to produce beyond its normal wont, then shouldn't we consider kindness as a tool to ward off Earth's hunger? How much more might be produced if the farmer loved his wheat?

It's silly, of course, a principle that could not gain acceptance.

And undoubtedly it would not work — not in a plant-utilizing culture.

For how could you keep on convincing a plant that you feel kindly toward it when, season after season, you prove that your only interest in it is to eat it or make it into clothing or chop it down for lumber?

I walked out back of the shed and stood beside the yellow rose, trying to find the answer. The yellow rose stirred, like a pretty woman who knows she's being admired, but no emotion came from it.

The thanks and happiness were gone. There was nothing left but the loneliness.

Damned vegetable aliens — upsetting a man so he couldn't eat his breakfast cereal in peace!

SMALL DEER

Willow Bend,
Wisconsin
June 23, 1966

Dr Wyman Jackson,
Wyalusing College,
Muscoda, Wisconsin

My dear Dr Jackson:

I am writing to you because I don't know who else to write to and there is something I have to tell someone who can understand. I know your name because I read your book, 'Cretaceous Dinosaurs,' not once, but many times. I tried to get Dennis to read it, too, but I guess he never did. All Dennis was interested in were the mathematics of his time concept — not the time machine itself. Besides, Dennis doesn't read too well. It is a chore for him.

Maybe I should tell you, to start with, that my name is Alton James. I live with my widowed mother and I run a fix-it shop. I fix bicycles and lawn mowers and radios and television sets — I fix anything that is brought to me. I'm not much good at anything else, but I do seem to have the knack of seeing how things go together and understanding how they work and seeing what is wrong with them when they aren't working. I never had no training of any sort,

65

but I just seem to have a natural bent for getting along with mechanical contraptions.

Dennis is my friend and I'll admit right off that he is a strange one. He doesn't know from nothing about anything, but he's nuts on mathematics. People in town make fun of him because he is so strange and Ma gives me hell at times for having anything to do with him. She says he's the next best thing to a village idiot. I guess a lot of people think the way that Ma does, but it is not entirely true, for he does know his math.

I don't know how he knows it. He didn't learn it at school and that's for sure. When he got to be 17 and hadn't got no farther than eighth grade, the school just sort of dropped him. He didn't really get to eighth grade honest; the teachers after a while got tired of seeing him on one grade and passed him to the next. There was talk, off and on, of sending him to some special school, but it never got nowhere.

And don't ask me what kind of mathematics he knew. I tried to read up on math once because I had the feeling, after seeing some of the funny marks that Dennis put on paper, that maybe he knew more about it than anyone else in the world. And I still think that he does – or that maybe he's invented an entirely new kind of math. For in the books I looked through I never did find any of the symbols that Dennis put on paper. Maybe Dennis used symbols he made up, inventing them as he went along, because no one had ever told him what the regular mathematicians used. But I don't think that's it – I'm inclined to lean to the idea Dennis came up with a new brand of math, entirely.

There were times I tried to talk with Dennis about this math of his and each time he was surprised that I didn't know it, too. I guess he thought most people knew about it. He said that it was simple, that it was plain as day. It was the way things worked, he said.

I suppose you'll want to ask how come I understood his equations well enough to make the time machine. The answer is I didn't. I suppose that Dennis and I are alike in a lot of ways, but in different ways. I know how to make contraptions work (without knowing any of the theory) and Dennis sees the entire universe as something operating mechanically (and him scarcely able to read a page of simple type).

And another thing. My family and Dennis' family live in the same end of town and from the time we were toddlers, Dennis and I played together. Later on, we just kept on together. We didn't have a choice. For some reason or other, none of the kids would play with us. Unless we wanted to play alone, we had to play together. I guess we got so, through the years, that we understood each other.

I don't suppose there'd have been any time machine if I hadn't been so interested in paleontology. Not that I knew anything about it; I was just interested. From the time I was a kid I read everything I could lay my hands on about dinosaurs and saber-tooths and such. Later on I went fossil hunting in the hills, but I never found nothing really big. Mostly I found brachiopods. There are great beds of them in the Platteville limestone. And lots of times I'd stand in the street and look up at the river bluffs above the town and try to imagine what it had been like a million years ago, or a hundred million. When I first read in a story about a time machine, I remember thinking how I'd like to have one. I guess that at one time I thought a little about making one, but then realized I couldn't.

Dennis had a habit of coming to my shop and talking, but most of the time talking to himself rather than to me. I don't remember exactly how it started, but after a while I realized that he had stopped talking about anything but time. One day he told me he had been able to figure out everything but time, and now it seemed he was getting that down in black and white, like all the rest of it.

Mostly I didn't pay too much attention to what he said, for a lot of it didn't make much sense. But after he'd talked, incessantly, for a week or two, on time, I began to pay attention. But don't expect me to tell you what he said or make any sense of it, for there's no way that I can. To understand what Dennis said and meant, you'd have to live with him, like I did, for twenty years or more. It's not so much understanding what Dennis says as understanding Dennis.

I don't think we actually made any real decision to build a time machine, it just sort of grew on us. All at once we found that we were making one.

We took our time. We had to take our time, for we went back a lot and did things over, almost from the start. It took weeks to get some of the proper effects — at least, that's what Dennis called them. Me, I didn't know anything about effects. All that I knew was that Dennis wanted to make something work a certain way and I tried to make it work that way. Sometimes, even when it worked the way he wanted it, it turned out to be wrong. So we'd start all over.

But finally we had a working model of it and took it out on a big bald bluff, several miles up the river, where no one ever went. I rigged up a timer to a switch that would turn it on, then after two minutes would reverse the field and send it home again.

We mounted a movie camera inside the frame that carried the machine, and we set the camera going, then threw the timer switch.

I had my doubts that it would work, but it did. It went away and stayed for two minutes, then came back again.

When we developed the camera film, we knew without any question the camera had traveled back in time. At first there were picutres of ourselves standing there and waiting. Then there was a little blur, no more than a flicker across a half a dozen frames, and the next frames showed a mastodon walking straight into the camera. A fraction of a second later his trunk jerked up and his ears flared out as he wheeled around with clumsy haste and galloped down the ridge.

Every now and then he'd swing his head around to take a look behind him. I imagine that our time machine, blossoming suddenly out of the ground in front of him, scared him out of seven years of growth.

We were lucky, that was all. We could have sent that camera back another thousand times, perhaps, and never caught a mastodon — probably never caught a thing. Although we would have known it had moved in time, for the landscape had been different, although not a great deal different, but from the landscape we could not have told if it had gone back a hundred or a thousand years. When we saw the mastodon, however, we knew we'd sent the camera back 10,000 years at least.

I won't bore you with how we worked out a lot of problems on our second model, or how Dennis managed to work out a time-meter that we could calibrate to send the machine a specific distance into time. Because all this is not important. What is important is what I found when I went into time.

I've already told you I'd read your book about Cretaceous dinosaurs and I liked the entire book, but that final chapter about the extinction of the dinosaurs is the one that really got me. Many a time I'd lie awake at night thinking about all the theories you wrote about and trying to figure out in my own mind how it really was.

So when it was time to get into that machine and go, I knew where I would be headed.

Dennis gave me no argument. He didn't even want to go. He didn't care no more. He never was really interested in the time machine. All he wanted was to prove out his math. Once the machine did that, he was through with it.

I worried a lot, going as far as I meant to go, about the rising or subsidence of the crust. I knew that the land around Willow Bend had been stable for millions of years. Sometime during the Cretaceous a sea had crept into the interior of the continent, but had stopped short of Wisconsin and, so far as geologists could determine, there had been no disturbances in the state. But I still felt uneasy about it. I didn't want to come out into the Late Cretaceous with the machine buried under a dozen feet of rock or, maybe, hanging a dozen feet up in the air.

So I got some heavy steel pipes and sunk them six feet into the rock on the bald bluff top we had used the first time, with about ten feet of their length extending in the air. I mounted the time frame on top of them and rigged up a ladder to get in and out of it and tied the pipes into the time field. One morning I packed a lunch and filled a canteen with water. I dug the old binoculars that had been my father's out of the attic and debated whether I should take along a gun. All I had was a shotgun and I decided not to take it. If I'd had a rifle, there'd been no question of my taking it, but I didn't have one. I could have borrowed one, but I didn't want to. I'd kept pretty quiet about what I was doing and I didn't want to start any gossip in the village.

I went up to the bluff top and climbed up to the frame and set the time-meter to 63½ million years into the past and then I turned her on. I didn't make any ceremony out of it. I just turned her on and went.

I told you about the little blur in the movie film and that's the best way, I suppose, to tell you how it was. There was this little blur, like a flickering twilight. Then it was sunlight once again and I was on the bluff top, looking out across the valley.

Except it wasn't a bluff top any longer, but only a high hill. And the valley was not the rugged, tree-choked, deeply cut valley I had always known, but a great green plain, a wide and shallow valley with a wide and sluggish river flowing at the far side of it. Far to the west I could see a shimmer in the sunlight, a large lake or sea. But a sea, I thought, shouldn't be this far east. But there it was, either a great lake or a sea – I never did determine which.

And there was something else as well. I looked down to the ground and it was only three feet under me. Was I ever glad I had used those pipes!

Looking out across the valley, I could see moving things, but they were so far away that I could not make them out.

So I picked up the binoculars and jumped down to the ground and walked across the hilltop until the ground began to slope away.

I sat down and put the binoculars to my eyes and worked across the valley with them.

There were dinosaurs out there, a whole lot more of them than I had expected. They were in herds and they were traveling. You'd expect that out of any dozen herds of them, some of them would be feeding, but none of them was. All of them were moving and it seemed to me there was a nervousness in the way they moved. Although, I told myself, that might be the way it was with dinosaurs.

They all were a long way off, even with the glasses, but I could make out some of them. There were several groups of duckbills, waddling along and making funny jerky movements with their heads. I spotted a couple of small herds of thescelosaurs, pacing along, with their bodies tilted forward. Here and there were small groups of triceratops. But strangest of all was a large herd of brontosaurs, ambling nervously and gingerly along, as if their feet might hurt. And it struck me strange, for they were a long way from water and from what I'd read in your book, and in other books, it didn't seem too likely they ever wandered too far away from water.

And there were a lot of other things that didn't look too much like the pictures I had seen in books.

The whole business had a funny feel about it. Could it be, I wondered, that I had stumbled on some great migration, with all the dinosaurs heading out for some place else?

I got so interested in watching that I was downright careless and it was foolish of me. I was in another world and there could have been all sorts of dangers and I should have been watching out for them, but I was just sitting there, flat upon my backside, as if I were at home.

Suddenly there was a pounding, as if someone had turned loose a piledriver, coming up behind me and coming very fast. I dropped the glasses and twisted around and as I did something big and tall rushed past me, no more than three feet away, so close it almost brushed me. I got just a brief impression of it as it went by – huge and gray and scaly.

Then, as it went tearing down the hill, I saw what it was and I had a cold and sinking feeling clear down in my gizzard. For I had been almost run down by the big boy of them all – Tyrannosaurus rex.

His two great legs worked like driving pistons and the light of the sun glinted off the wicked, recurved claws as his feet pumped up and down. His tail rode low and awkward, but there was no awkwardness in the way he moved. His monstrous head swung from side to side, with the great rows of teeth showing in the gaping mouth, and he left behind him a faint foul smell – I suppose from the carrion he ate. But the big surprise was that the wattles hanging underneath his throat were a brilliant iridescence – red and green and gold and purple, the color of them shifting as he swung his head.

I watched him for just a second and them I jumped up and headed for the time machine. I was more scared than I like to think about. I had, I want to testify right here, seen enough of dinosaurs for a lifetime.

But I never reached the time machine.

Up over the brow of the hill came something else. I say something else because I have no idea what it really was. Not as big as rex, but ten times worse than him.

It was long and sinuous and it had a lot of legs and it stood six feet high or so and was a sort of sickish pink. Take a caterpillar and magnify it until it's six feet tall, then give it longer legs so that it can run instead of crawl and hang a death mask dragon's head upon it and you get a faint idea. Just a faint idea.

It saw me and swung its head toward me and made an eager whimpering sound and it slid along toward me with a side-wheeling gait, like a dog when it's running out of balance and lop-sided.

I took one look at it and dug in my heels and made so

sharp a turn that I lost my hat. The next thing I knew, I was pelting down the hill behind old Tyrannosaurus.

And now I saw that myself and rex were not the only things that were running down the hill. Scattered here and there along the hillside were other running creatures, most of them in small groups and herds, although there were some singles. Most of them were dinosaurs, but there were other things as well.

I'm sorry I can't tell you what they were, but at that particular moment I wasn't what you might call an astute observer. I was running for my life, as if the flames of hell were lapping at my heels.

I looked around a couple of times and that sinuous creature was still behind me. He wasn't gaining on me any, although I had the feeling that he could if he put his mind to it. Matter of fact, he didn't seem to be following me alone. He was doing a lot of weaving back and forth. He reminded me of nothing quite so much as a faithful farm dog bringing in the cattle. But even thinking this, it took me a little time to realize that was exactly what he was – an old farm dog bringing in a bunch of assorted dinosaurs and one misplaced human being. At the bottom of the hill I looked back again and now that I could see the whole slope of the hill, I saw that this was a bigger cattle drive than I had imagined. The entire hill was alive with running beasts and behind them were a half dozen of the pinkish dogs.

And I knew when I saw this that the moving herds I'd seen out on the valley floor were not migratory herds, but they were moving because they were being driven – that this was a big roundup of some sort, with all the reptiles and the dinosaurs and myself being driven to a common center.

I knew that my life depended on getting lost somehow, and being left behind. I had to find a place to hide and I had to dive into this hiding place without being seen. Only trouble was there seemed no place to hide. The valley floor was naked and nothing bigger than a mouse could have hidden there.

Ahead of me a good-size swale rose up from the level floor and I went pelting up it. I was running out of wind. My breath was getting short and I had pains throbbing in my chest and I knew I couldn't run much farther.

I reached the top of the swale and started down the reverse slope. And there, right in front of me, was a bush of some sort, three feet high or so, bristling with thorns. I was too close to it and going too fast to even try to dodge it, so I did the only thing I could – I jumped over it.

But on the other side there was no solid ground. There was, instead, a hole. I caught just a glimpse of it and tried to jerk my body to one side, and then I was falling into the hole.

It wasn't much bigger than I was. It bumped me as I fell and I picked up some bruises, then landed with a jolt. The fall knocked the breath out of me and I was doubled over, with my arms wrapped about my belly.

My breath came slowly back and the pain subsided and I was able to take a look at where I was.

The hole was some three feet in diameter and perhaps as much as seven deep. It slanted slightly toward the forefront of the slope and its sides were worn smooth. A thin trickle of dirt ran down from the edge of it, soil that I had loosened and dislodged when I had hit the hole. And about halfway up was a cluster of small rocks, the largest of them about the size of a human head, projecting more than half their width out of the wall. I thought, idly, as I looked at them, that some day they'd come loose and drop into the hole. And at the thought I squirmed around a little to one side, so that if they took a notion to fall I'd not be in the line of fire.

Looking down, I saw that I'd not fallen to the bottom of the hole, for the hole went on, deeper in the ground. I had come to rest at a point where the hole curved sharply, to angle back beneath the swale top.

I hadn't noticed it at first, I suppose because I had been too shook up, but now I became aware of a musky smell.

Not an overpowering odor, but a sort of scent — faintly animal, although not quite animal.

A smooth-sided hole and a musky smell — there could be no other answer: I had fallen not into just an ordinary hole but into a burrow of some sort. And it must be the burrow of quite an animal, I thought, to be the size it was. It would have taken something with hefty claws, indeed, to have dug this sort of burrow.

And even as I thought it, I heard the rattling and the scrabbling of something coming up the burrow, no doubt coming up to find out what was going on.

I did some scrabbling myself. I didn't waste no time. But about three feet up I slipped. I grabbed for the top of the hole, but my fingers slid through the sandy soil and I couldn't get a grip. I shot out my feet and stopped my slide short of the bottom of the hole. And there I was, with my back against one side of the hole and my feet braced against the other, hanging there, halfway up the burrow.

While all the time below me the scrabbling and the clicking sounds continued. The thing, whatever it might be, was getting closer, and it was coming fast.

Right in front of me was the nest of rocks sticking from the wall. I reached out and grabbed the biggest one and jerked and it came loose. It was heavier than I had figured it would be and I almost dropped it, but managed to hang on.

A snout came out of the curve in the burrow and thrust itself quickly upward in a grabbing motion. The jaws opened up and they almost filled the burrow and they were filled with sharp and wicked teeth.

I didn't think. I didn't plan. What I did was instinct. I dropped the rock between my spread-out legs straight down into that gaping maw. It was a heavy rock and it dropped four feet or so and went straight between the teeth, down into the blackness of the throat. When it hit it splashed and the jaws snapped shut and the creature backed away.

How I did it, I don't know, but I got out of the hole. I

clawed and kicked against the wall and heaved my body up and rolled out of the hole onto the naked hillside.

Naked, that is, except for the bush with the inch-long thorns, the one that I'd jumped over before I fell into the burrow. It was the only cover there was and I made for the upper side of it, for by now, I figured, the big cattle drive had gone past me and if I could get the bush between myself and the valley side of the swale, I might have a chance. Otherwise, sure as hell, one of those dogs would see me and would come out to bring me in.

For while there was no question that they were dinosaur herders, they probably couldn't tell the difference between me and a dinosaur. I was alive and could run and that would qualify me.

There was always the chance, of course, that the owner of the burrow would come swarming out, and if he did I couldn't stay behind the bush. But I rather doubted he'd be coming out, not right away, at least. It would take him a while to get that stone out of his throat.

I crouched behind the bush and the sun was hot upon my back and, peering through the branches, I could see, far out on the valley floor, the great herd of milling beasts. All of them had been driven together and there they were, running in a knotted circle, while outside the circle prowled the pinkish dogs and something else as well – what appeared to be men driving tiny cars. The cars and men were all of the same color, a sort of greenish gray, and the two of them, the cars and men, seemed to be a single organism. The men didn't seem to be sitting in the cars; they looked as if they grew out of the cars, as if they and the cars were one. And while the cars went zipping along, they appeared to have no wheels. It was hard to tell, but they seemed to travel with the bottom of them flat upon the ground, like a snail would travel, and as they traveled, they rippled, as if the body of the car were some sort of flowing muscle.

I crouched there watching and now, for the first time, I had a chance to think about it, to try to figure out what was going on. I had come here, across more than sixty million years, to see some dinosaurs, and I sure was seeing them, but under what you might say were peculiar circumstances. The dinosaurs fit, all right. They looked mostly like the way they looked in books, but the dogs and car-men were something else again. They were distinctly out of place.

The dogs were pacing back and forth, sliding along in their sinuous fashion, and the car-men were zipping back and forth, and every once in a while one of the beasts would break out of the circle and the minute that it did, a half dozen dogs and a couple of car-men would race to intercept it and drive it back again.

The circle of beasts must have had, roughly, a diameter of a mile or more – a mile of milling, frightened creatures. A lot of paleontologists have wondered whether dinosaurs had any voice and I can tell you that they did. They were squealing and roaring and quacking and there were some of them that hooted – I think it was the duckbills hooting, but I can't be sure.

Then, all at once, there was another sound, a sort of fluttering roar that seemed to be coming from the sky. I looked up quickly and I saw them coming down – a dozen or so spaceships, they couldn't have been anything but spaceships. They came down rather fast and they didn't seem too big and there were tails of thin, blue flame flickering at their bases. Not the billowing clouds of flame and smoke that our rockets have, but just a thin blue flicker.

For a minute it looked like one of them would land on top of me, but then I saw that it was too far out. It missed me, matter of fact, a good two miles or so. It and the others sat down in a ring around the milling herd out in the valley.

I should have known what would happen out there. It was the simplest explanation one could think of and it was logical. I think, maybe, way deep down, I did know, but

77

my surface mind had pushed it away because it was too matter-of-fact and too ordinary.

Thin snouts spouted from the ships and purple fire curled mistily at the muzzle of those snouts and the dinosaurs went down in a fighting, frightened, squealing mass. Thin trickles of vapor drifted upward from the snouts and out in the center of the circle lay that heap of dead and dying dinosaurs, all those thousands of dinosaurs piled in death.

It is a simple thing to tell, of course, but it was a terrible thing to see. I crouched there behind the bush, sickened at the sight, startled by the silence when all the screaming and the squealing and the hooting ceased. And shaken, too – not by what shakes me now as I write this letter, but shaken by the knowledge that something from outside could do this to the Earth.

For they were from outside. It wasn't just the spaceships, but those pinkish dogs and gray-green car men, which were not cars and men, but a single organism, were not things of Earth, could not be things of Earth.

I crept back from the bush, keeping low in hope that the bush would screen me from the things down in the valley until I reached the swale top. One of the dogs swung around and looked my way and I froze, and after a time he looked away.

Then I was over the top of the swale and heading back toward the time machine. But half way down the slope, I turned around and came back again, crawling on my belly, squirming to the hilltop to have another look.

It was a look I'll not forget.

The dogs and car-men had swarmed in upon the heap of dead dinosaurs, and some of the cars already were crawling back toward the grounded spaceships, which had let down ramps. The cars were moving slowly, for they were heavily loaded and the loads they carried were neatly butchered hams and racks of ribs.

And in the sky there was a muttering and I looked up to see yet other spaceships coming down – the little transport ships that would carry this cargo of fresh meat up to another larger ship that waited overhead.

It was then I turned and ran.

I reached the top of the hill and piled into the time machine and set it at zero and came home. I didn't even stop to hunt for the binoculars I'd dropped.

And now that I am home, I'm not going back again. I'm not going anywhere in that time machine. I'm afraid of what I might find any place I go. If Wyalusing College has any need of it, I'll give them the time machine.

But that's not why I wrote.

There is no doubt in my mind what happened to the dinosaurs, why they became extinct. They were killed off and butchered and hauled away, to some other planet, perhaps many light years distant, by a race which looked upon the earth as a cattle range – a planet that could supply a vast amount of cheap protein.

But that, you say, happened more than sixty million years ago. This race did once exist. But in sixty million years it would almost certainly have changed its ways or drifted off in its hunting to some other sector of the galaxy, or, perhaps, have become extinct, like the dinosaurs.

But I don't think so. I don't think any of those things happened. I think they're still around. I think Earth may be only one of many planets which supply their food.

And I'll tell you why I think so. They were back on Earth again, I'm sure, some 10,000 or 11,000 years ago, when they killed off the mammoth and the mastodon, the giant bison, the great cave bear and the saber-tooth and a lot of other things. Oh, yes, I know they missed Africa. They never touched the big game there. Maybe, after wiping out the dinosaurs, they learned their lesson, and left Africa for breeding stock.

And now I come to the point of this letter, the thing that has me worried.

Today there are just a few less than three billion of us humans in the world. By the year 2000 there may be as many as six billion of us.

We're pretty small, of course, and these things went in for tonnage, for dinosaurs and mastodon and such. But there are so many of us! Small as we are, we may be getting to the point where we'll be worth their while.

THE GHOST OF A MODEL T

He was walking home when he heard the Model T again. It was not a sound that he could well mistake, and it was not the first time he had heard it running, in the distance, on the road. Although it puzzled him considerably, for so far as he knew, no one in the country had a Model T. He'd read somewhere, in a paper more than likely, that old cars, such as Model T's, were fetching a good price, although why this should be, he couldn't figure out. With all the smooth, sleek cars that there were today, who in their right mind would want a Model T? But there was no accounting, in these crazy times, for what people did. It wasn't like the old days, but the old days were long gone, and a man had to get along the best he could with the way that things were now.

Brad had closed up the beer joint early, and there was no place to go but home, although since Old Bounce had died he rather dreaded to go home. He certainly did miss Bounce, he told himself; they'd got along just fine, the two of them, for more than twenty years, but now, with the old dog gone, the house was a lonely place and had an empty sound.

He walked along the dirt road out at the edge of town, his feet scuffing in the dust and kicking at the clods. The night was almost as light as day, with a full moon above the treetops. Lonely cricket noises were heralding summer's end. Walking along, he got to remembering the Model T he'd had when he'd been a young sprout, and how he'd spent hours out in the old machine shed tuning it up, although, God knows, no Model T ever really needed tuning. It was about as simple a piece of mechanism as anyone could want, and despite some technological cantankerousness, about as faithful a car as ever had been built. It got you there and got you back, and that was all, in those days, that anyone could ask. Its fenders rattled, and its hard tires bounced, and it could be balky on a hill, but if you knew how to handle it and mother it along, you never had no trouble.

Those were the days, he told himself, when everything had been as simple as a Model T. There were no income taxes (although, come to think of it, for him, personally, income taxes had never been a problem), no social security that took part of your wages, no licensing this and that, no laws that said a beer joint had to close at a certain hour. It had been easy, then, he thought; a man just fumbled along the best way he could, and there was no one telling him what to do or getting in his way.

The sound of the Model T, he realized, had been getting louder all the time, although he had been so busy with his thinking that he'd paid no real attention to it. But now, from the sound of it, it was right behind him, and although he knew it must be his imagination, the sound was so natural and so close that he jumped to one side of the road so it wouldn't hit him.

It came up beside him and stopped, and there it was, as big as life, and nothing wrong with it. The front-right-hand door (the only door in front, for there was no door on the left-hand side) flapped open – just flapped open by itself, for there was no one in the car to open it. The door flapping open didn't surprise him any, for to his recollection, no one who owned a Model T ever had been able to keep that front door closed. It was held only by a simple latch, and every time the car bounced (and there was seldom a time it wasn't bouncing, considering the condition of the roads in those days, the hardness of the tires, and the construction of the springs) — every time the car bounced, that damn front door came open.

This time, however — after all these years — there seemed to be something special about how the door came open. It seemed to be a sort of invitation, the car coming to a stop and the door not just sagging open, but coming open with a flourish, as if it were inviting him to step inside the car.

So he stepped inside of it and sat down on the right-front seat, and as soon as he was inside, the door closed and the car began rolling down the road. He started moving over to get behind the wheel, for there was no one driving it, and a curve was coming up, and the car needed someone to steer it around the curve. But before he could move over and get his hands upon the wheel, the car began to take the curve as neatly as it would have with someone driving it. He sat astonished and did not touch the wheel, and it went around the curve without even hesitating, and beyond the curve was a long, steep hill, and the engine labored mightily to achieve the speed to attack the hill.

The funny thing about it, he told himself, still half-crouched to take the wheel and still not touching it, was that he knew this road by heart, and there was no curve or hill on it. The road ran straight for almost three miles before it joined the River Road, and there was not a curve or kink in it, and certainly no hill. But there had been a curve, and there was a hill, for the car laboring up it quickly lost its speed and had to shift to low.

Slowly he straightened up and slid over to the right-hand side of the seat, for it was quite apparent that this Model T, for whatever reason, did not need a driver — perhaps did better with no driver. It seemed to know where it was going, and he told himself, this was more than he knew, for the country, while vaguely familiar, was not the country that lay about the little town of Willow Bend. It was rough and hilly country, and Willow Bend lay on a flat, wide floodplain of the river, and there were no hills and no rough ground until you reached the distant bluffs that stood above the valley.

He took off his cap and let the wind blow through his hair, and there was nothing to stop the wind, for the top of the car was down. The car gained the top of the hill and started going down, wheeling carefully back and forth down the switchbacks that followed the contour of the hill. Once it started down, it shut off the ignition somehow, just the way he used to do, he remembered, when he drove his Model T. The cylinders slapped and slobbered prettily, and the engine cooled.

As the car went around a looping bend that curved above a deep, black hollow that ran between the hills, he caught the fresh, sweet scent of fog, and that scent woke old memories in him, and if he'd not known differently, he would have thought he was back in the country of his young manhood. For in the wooded hills where he'd grown up, fog came creeping up a valley of a summer evening, carrying with it the smells of cornfields and of clover pastures and many other intermingled scents abstracted from a fat and fertile land. But it could not be, he knew, the country of his early years, for that country lay far off and was not to be reached in less than an hour of travel. Although he was somewhat puzzled by exactly where he could be, for it did not seem the kind of country that could be found within striking distance of the town of Willow Bend.

The car came down off the hill and ran blithely up a valley road. It passed a farmhouse huddled up against the hill, with two lighted windows gleaming, and off to one side the shadowy shapes of barn and henhouse. A dog came out and barked at them. There had been no other houses, although, far off, on the opposite hills, he had seen a pinpoint of light here and there and was sure that they were farms. Nor had they met any other cars, although, come to think of it, that was not so strange, for out here in the farming country there were late chores to do, and bedtime came early for people who were out at the crack of dawn. Except on weekends, there'd not be much traffic on a country road.

The Model T swung around a curve, and there, up ahead, was a garish splash of light, and as they came closer, music could be heard. There was about it all an old familiarity that nagged at him, but as yet he could not tell why it seemed familiar. The Model T slowed and turned in at the splash of light, and now it was clear that the light came from a dance pavilion. Strings of bulbs ran across its front, and other lights were mounted on tall poles in the parking area. Through the lighted windows he could see the dancers; and the music, he realized, was the kind of music he'd not heard for more than half a century. The Model T ran smoothly into a parking spot beside a Maxwell touring car. A Maxwell touring car, he thought with some surprise. There hadn't been a Maxwell on the road for years. Old Virg once had owned a Maxwell, at the same time he had owned his Model T. Old Virg, he thought. So many years ago. He tried to recall Old Virg's last name, but it wouldn't come to him. Of late, it seemed, names were often hard to come by. His name had been Virgil, but his friends always called him Virg. They'd been together quite a lot, the two of them, he remembered, running off to dances, drinking moonshine whiskey, playing pool, chasing girls – all the things that young sprouts did when they had the time and money.

He opened the door and got out of the car, the crushed gravel of the parking lot crunching underneath his feet; and the crunching of the gravel triggered the recognition of the place, supplied the reason for the familiarity that had first eluded him. He stood stock-still, half-frozen at the knowledge, looking at the ghostly leafiness of the towering elm trees that grew to either side of the dark bulk of the pavilion. His eyes took in the contour of the looming hills, and he recognized the contour, and standing there, straining for the sound, he heard the gurgle of the rushing water that came out of the hill, flowing through a wooden channel into a wayside watering trough that was now falling apart with neglect, no longer needed since the automobile had taken over from the horse-drawn vehicles of some years before.

He turned and sat down weakly on the running board of the Model T. His eyes could not deceive him or his ears betray him. He'd heard the distinctive sound of that running water too often in years long past to mistake it now; and the loom of the elm trees, the contour of the hills, the graveled parking lot, the string of bulbs on the pavilion's front, taken all together, could only mean that somehow he had returned or been returned, to Big Spring Pavilion. But that, he told himself, was fifty years or more ago, when I was lithe and young, when Old Virg had his Maxwell and I my Model T.

He found within himself a growing excitement that surged above the wonder and the sense of absurd impossibility – an excitement that was as puzzling as the place itself and his being there again. He rose and walked across the parking lot, with the coarse gravel rolling and sliding and crunching underneath his feet, and there was a strange lightness in his body, the kind of youthful lightness he had not known for years, and as the music came welling out at him, he found that he was gliding and turning to the music. Not the kind of music the kids played nowadays, with all the racket amplified by electronic contraptions, not the grating, no-rhythm junk that set one's teeth on edge and turned the morons glassy-eyed, but music with a beat to it, music you could dance to with a certain haunting quality that was no longer heard. The saxophone sounded clear, full-throated; and a sax, he told himself, was an instrument all but forgotten now. But it was here, and the music to go with it, and the bulbs above the door swaying in the little breeze that came drifting up the valley.

He was halfway through the door when he suddenly remembered that the pavilion was not free, and he was about to get some change out of his pocket (what little there was left after all those beers he'd had at Brad's) when he noticed the inky marking of the stamp on the back of his right hand. That had been the way, he remembered, that they'd marked you as having paid your way into the pavilion, a stamp placed on your hand. He showed his hand with its inky marking to the man who stood beside the door and went on in. The pavilion was bigger than he'd remembered it. The band sat on a raised platform to one side, and the floor was filled with dancers.

The years fell away, and it all was as he remembered it. The girls wore pretty dresses; there was not a single one who was dressed in jeans. The boys wore ties and jackets, and there was a decorum and a jauntiness that he had forgotten. The man who played the saxophone stood up, and the sax wailed in lonely melody, and there was a magic in the place that he had thought no longer could exist.

He moved out into the magic. Without knowing that he was about to do it, surprised when he found himself doing it, he was out on the floor, dancing by himself, dancing with all the other dancers, sharing in the magic – after all the lonely years, a part of it again. The best of the music filled the world, and all the world drew in to center on the dance floor, and although there was no girl and he danced all by himself, he remembered all the girls he had ever danced with.

Someone laid a heavy hand on his arm, and someone else was saying, 'Oh, for Christ's sake, leave the old guy be; he's just having fun like all the rest of us.' The heavy hand was jerked from his arm, and the owner of the heavy hand went staggering out across the floor, and there was a sudden flurry of activity that could not be described as dancing. A girl grabbed him by the hand. 'Come on, Pop,' she said, 'let's get out of here.' Someone else was pushing at his back to force him in the direction that the girl was pulling, and then he was out-of-doors. 'You better get on your way, Pop,' said a young man. 'They'll be calling the police. Say, what is your name? Who are you?'

'I am Hank,' he said. 'My name is Hank, and I used to come here. Me and Old Virg. We came here a lot. I got a Model T out in the lot if you want a lift.'

'Sure, why not,' said the girl. 'We are coming with you.'

He led the way, and they came behind him, and all piled in the car, and there were more of them than he had thought there were. They had to sit on one another's laps to make room in the car. He sat behind the wheel, but he never touched it, for he knew the Model T would know what was expected of it, and of course it did. It started up and wheeled out of the lot and headed for the road.

'Here, Pop,' said the boy who sat beside him, 'have a snort. It ain't the best there is, but it's got a wallop. It won't poison you; it ain't poisoned any of the rest of us.'

Hank took the bottle and put it to his lips. He tilted up his head and let the bottle gurgle. And if there'd been any doubt before of where he was, the liquor settled all the doubt. For the taste of it was a taste that could never be forgotten. Although it could not be remembered, either. A man had to taste it once again to remember it.

He took down the bottle and handed it to the one who had given it to him. 'Good stuff,' he said.

'Not good,' said the young man, 'but the best that we could get. These bootleggers don't give a damn what they sell you. Way to do it is to make them take a drink before you buy it, then watch them for a while. If they don't fall down dead or get blind staggers, then it's safe to drink.'

Reaching from the back seat of the car, one of them handed him a saxophone. 'Pop, you look like a man who could play this thing,' said one of the girls, 'so give us some music.'

'Where'd you get this thing?' asked Hank.

'We got it off the band,' said a voice from the back. 'That joker who was playing it had no right to have it. He was just abusing it.'

Hank put it to his lips and fumbled at the keys, and all at once the instrument was making music. And it was funny, he thought, for until right now he'd never held any kind of horn. He had no music in him. He'd tried a mouth organ once, thinking it might help to pass away the time, but the sounds that had come out of it had set

Old Bounce to howling. So he'd put it up on a shelf and had forgotten it till now.

The Model T went tooling down the road, and in a little time the pavilion was left behind. Hank tootled on the saxophone, astonishing himself at how well he played, while the others sang and passed around the bottle. There were no other cars on the road, and soon the Model T climbed a hill out of the valley and ran along a ridgetop, with all the countryside below a silver dream flooded by the moonlight.

Later on, Hank wondered how long this might have lasted, with the car running through the moonlight on the ridgetop, with him playing the saxophone, interrupting the music only when he laid aside the instrument to have another drink of moon. But when he tried to think of it, it seemed to have gone on forever, with the car eternally running in the moonlight, trailing behind it the wailing and the honking of the saxophone.

He woke to night again. The same full moon was shining, although the Model T had pulled off the road and was parked beneath a tree, so that the full strength of the moonlight did not fall upon him. He worried rather feebly if this might be the same night or a different night, and there was no way for him to tell, although, he told himself, it didn't make much difference. So long as the moon was shining and he had the Model T and a road for it to run on, there was nothing more to ask, and which night it was had no consequence.

The young people who had been with him were no longer there, but the saxophone was laid upon the floor-boards, and when he pulled himelf erect, he heard a gurgle in his pocket, and upon investigation, pulled out the moonshine bottle. It still was better than half full, and from the amount of drinking that had been done, that seemed rather strange.

He sat quietly behind the wheel, looking at the bottle in his hand, trying to decide if he should have a drink. He decided that he shouldn't, and put the bottle back into his pocket, then reached down and got the saxophone and laid it on the seat beside him.

The Model T stirred to life, coughing and stuttering. It inched forward, somewhat reluctantly, moving from beneath the tree, heading in a broad sweep for the road. It reached the road and went bumping down it. Behind it a thin cloud of dust, kicked up by its heels, hung silver in the moonlight.

Hank sat proudly behind the wheel, being careful not to touch it. He folded his hands in his lap and leaned back. He felt good – the best he'd ever felt. Well, maybe not the best, he told himself, for back in the time of youth, when he was spry and limber and filled with the juice of hope, there might have been some times when he felt as good as he felt now. His mind went back, searching for the times when he'd felt as good, and out of olden memory came another time, when he'd drunk just enough to give himself an edge, not as yet verging into drunkenness, not really wanting any more to drink, and he'd stood on the gravel of the Big Spring parking lot, listening to the music before going in, with the bottle tucked inside his shirt, cold against his belly. The day had been a scorcher, and he'd been working in the hayfield, but now the night was cool, with fog creeping up the valley, carrying that indefinable scent of the fat and fertile land; and inside, the music playing, and a waiting girl who would have an eye out for the door, waiting for the moment he came in.

It had been good, he thought, that moment snatched out of the maw of time, but no better than this moment, with the car running on the ridgetop road and all the world laid out in the moonlight. Different, maybe, in some ways, but no better than this moment.

The road left the ridgetop and went snaking down the bluff face, heading for the valley floor. A rabbit hopped across the road, caught for a second in the feeble headlights. High in the nighttime sky, invisible, a bird cried out, but that was the only sound there was, other than the thumping and the clanking of the Model T.

The car went skittering down the valley, and here the

moonlight often was shut out by the woods that came down close against the road.

Then it was turning off the road, and beneath its tires he heard the crunch of gravel, and ahead of him loomed a dark and crouching shape. The car came to a halt, and sitting rigid in the seat, Hank knew where he was.

The Model T had returned to the dance pavilion, but the magic was gone. There were no lights, and it was deserted. The parking lot was empty. In the silence, as the Model T shut off its engine, he heard the gushing of the water from the hillside spring running into the watering trough.

Suddenly he felt cold and apprehensive. It was lonely here, lonely as only an old remembered place can be when all its life is gone. He stirred reluctantly and climbed out of the car, standing beside it, with one hand resting on it, wondering why the Model T had come here and why he'd gotten out.

A dark figure moved out from the front of the pavilion, an undistinguishable figure slouching in the darkness.

'That you, Hank?' a voice asked.

'Yes, it's me,' said Hank.

'Christ,' the voice asked, 'where is everybody?'

'I don't know,' said Hank. 'I was here just the other night. There were a lot of people then.'

The figure came closer. 'You wouldn't have a drink, would you?' it asked.

'Sure, Virg,' he said, for now he recognized the voice. 'Sure, I have a drink.'

He reached into his pocket and pulled out the bottle. He handed it to Virg. Virg took it and sat down on the running board. He didn't drink right away, but sat there cuddling the bottle.

'How you been, Hank?' he asked. 'Christ, it's a long time since I seen you.'

'I'm all right,' said Hank. 'I drifted up to Willow Bend and just sort of stayed there. You know Willow Bend?'

'I was through it once. Just passing through. Never stopped or nothing. Would have if I'd known you were there. I lost all track of you.'

There was something that Hank had heard about Old Virg, and felt that maybe he should mention it, but for the life of him he couldn't remember what it was, so he couldn't mention it.

'Things didn't go so good for me,' said Virg. 'Not what I had expected. Janet up and left me, and I took to drinking after that and lost the filling station. Then I just knocked around from one thing to another. Never could get settled. Never could latch onto anything worthwhile.'

He uncorked the bottle and had himself a drink.

'Good stuff,' he said, handing the bottle back to Hank.

Hank had a drink, then sat down on the running board alongside Virg and set the bottle down between them.

'I had a Maxwell for a while,' said Virg, 'but I seem to have lost it. Forgot where I left it, and I've looked everywhere.'

'You don't need your Maxwell, Virg,' said Hank. 'I have got this Model T.'

'Christ, it's lonesome here,' said Virg. 'Don't you think it's lonesome?'

'Yes, it's lonesome. Here, have another drink. We'll figure what to do.'

'It ain't good sitting here,' said Virg. 'We should get out among them.'

'We'd better see how much gas we have,' said Hank. 'I don't know what's in the tank.'

He got up and opened the front door and put his hand under the front seat, searching for the measuring stick. He found it and unscrewed the gas-tank cap. He began looking through his pockets for matches so he could make a light.

'Here,' said Virg, 'don't go lighting any matches near that tank. You'll blow us all to hell. I got a flashlight here in my back pocket. If the damn thing's working.'

The batteries were weak, but it made a feeble light. Hank plunged the stick into the tank, pulled it out when it hit bottom, holding his thumb on the point that marked the topside of the tank. The stick was wet up almost to his thumb.

'Almost full,' said Virg. 'When did you fill it last?'

'I ain't never filled it.'

Old Virg was impressed. 'That old tin lizard,' he said, 'sure goes easy on the gas.'

Hank screwed the cap back on the tank, and they sat down on the running board again, and each had another drink.

'It seems to me it's been lonesome for a long time now,' said Virg. 'Awful dark and lonesome. How about you, Hank?'

'I been lonesome,' said Hank, 'ever since Old Bounce up and died on me. I never did get married. Never got around to it. Bounce and me, we went everywhere together. He'd go up to Brad's bar with me and camp out underneath a table; then, when Brad threw us out, he'd walk home with me.'

'We ain't doing ourselves no good,' said Virg, 'just sitting here and moaning. So let's have another drink, then I'll crank the car for you, and we'll be on our way.'

'You don't need to crank the car,' said Hank. 'You just get into it, and it starts up by itself.'

'Well, I be damned,' said Virg. 'You sure have got it trained.'

They had another drink and got into the Model T, which started up and swung out of the parking lot, heading for the road.

'Where do you think we should go?' asked Virg. 'You know of any place to go?'

'No, I don't,' said Hank. 'Let the car take us where it wants to. It will know the way.'

Virg lifted the sax off the seat and asked, 'Where'd this thing come from? I don't remember you could blow a sax.'

'I never could before,' said Hank. He took the sax from Virg and put it to his lips, and it wailed in anguish, gurgled with light-heartedness.

'I be damned,' said Virg. 'You do it pretty good.'

The Model T bounced merrily down the road, with its fenders flapping and the windshield jiggling, while the magneto coils mounted on the dashboard clicked and clacked and chattered. All the while, Hank kept blowing on the sax and the music came out loud and true, with startled night birds squawking and swooping down to fly across the narrow swath of light.

The Model T went clanking up the valley road and climbed the hill to come out on a ridge, running through the moonlight on a narrow, dusty road between close pasture fences, with sleepy cows watching them pass by.

'I be damned,' cried Virg, 'if it isn't just like it used to be. The two of us together, running in the moonlight. Whatever happened to us, Hank? Where did we miss out? It's like this now, and it was like this a long, long time ago. Whatever happened to the years between? Why did there have to be any years between?'

Hank said nothing. He just kept blowing on the sax.

'We never asked for nothing much,' said Virg. 'We were happy as it was. We didn't ask for change. But the old crowd grew away from us. They got married and got steady jobs, and some of them got important. And that was the worst of all, when they got important. We were left alone. Just the two of us, just you and I, the ones who didn't want to change. It wasn't just being young that we were hanging on to. It was something else. It was a time that went with being young and crazy. I think we knew it somehow. And we were right, of course. It was never quite as good again.'

The Model T left the ridge and plunged down a long, steep hill, and below them they could see a massive highway, broad and many-laned, with many car lights moving on it.

'We're coming to a freeway, Hank,' said Virg. 'Maybe we should sort of veer away from it. This old Model T of yours is a good car, sure, the best there ever was, but that's fast company down there.'

'I ain't doing nothing to it,' said Hank. 'I ain't steering it. It is on its own. It knows what it wants to do.'

'Well, all right, what the hell,' said Virg, 'we'll ride along with it. That's all right with me. I feel safe with it. Comfortable with it. I never felt so comfortable in all my

94

goddamn life. Christ, I don't know what I'd done if you hadn't come along. Why don't you lay down that silly sax and have a drink before I drink it all.'

So Hank laid down the sax and had a couple of drinks to make up for lost time, and by the time he handed the bottle back to Virg, the Model T had gone charging up a ramp, and they were on the freeway. It went running gaily down its lane, and it passed some cars that were far from standing still. Its fenders rattled at a more rapid rate, and the chattering of the magneto coils was like machine-gun fire.

'Boy,' said Virg admiringly, 'see the old girl go. She's got life left in her yet. Do you have any idea, Hank, where we might be going?'

'Not the least,' said Hank, picking up the sax again.

'Well, hell,' said Virg, 'it don't really matter, just so we're on our way. There was a sign back there a ways that said Chicago. Do you think we could be headed for Chicago?'

Hank took the sax out of his mouth. 'Could be,' he said. 'I ain't worried over it.'

'I ain't worried neither,' said Old Virg. 'Chicago, here we come! Just so the booze holds out. It seems to be holding out. We've been sucking at it regular, and it's still better than half-full.'

'You hungry, Virg?' asked Hank.

'Hell, no,' said Virg. 'Not hungry, and not sleepy, either. I never felt so good in all my life. Just so the booze holds out and this heap hangs together.'

The Model T banged and clattered, running with a pack of smooth, sleek cars that did not bang and clatter, with Hank playing on the saxophone and Old Virg waving the bottle high and yelling whenever the rattling old machine outdistanced a Lincoln or a Cadillac. The moon hung in the sky and did not seem to move. The freeway became a throughway, and the first toll booth loomed ahead.

'I hope you got change,' said Virg. 'Myself, I am cleaned out.'

But no change was needed, for when the Model T came

near, the toll-gate arm moved up and let it go thumping through without payment.

'We got it made,' yelled Virg. 'The road is free for us, and that's the way it should be. After all you and I been through, we got something coming to us.'

Chicago loomed ahead, off to their left, with night lights gleaming in the towers that rose along the lakeshore, and they went around it in a long, wide sweep, and New York was just beyond the fishhook bend as they swept around Chicago and the lower curve of the lake.

'I never saw New York,' said Virg, 'but seen pictures of Manhattan and that can't be nothing but Manhattan. I never did know, Hank, that Chicago and Manhattan were so close together.'

'Neither did I,' said Hank, pausing from his tootling on the sax. 'The geography's all screwed up for sure, but what the hell do we care? With this rambling wreck, the whole damn world is ours.'

He went back to the sax, and the Model T kept rambling on. They went thundering through the canyons of Manhattan and circumnavigated Boston and went on down to Washington, where the Washington Monument stood up high and Old Abe sat brooding on Potomac's shore.

They went on down to Richmond and skated past Atlanta and skimmed along the moon-drenched sands of Florida. They ran along old roads where trees dripped Spanish moss and saw the lights of Old N'Orleans way off to their left. Now they were heading north again, and the car was galumphing along a ridgetop with neat farming country all spread out below them. The moon still stood where it had been before, hanging at the selfsame spot. They were moving through a world where it was always three A.M.

'You know,' said Virg, 'I wouldn't mind if this kept on forever. I wouldn't mind if we never got to wherever we are going. It's too much fun getting there to worry where we're headed. Why don't you lay down that horn and have another drink? You must be getting powerful dry.'

Hank put down the sax and reached out for the bottle.

'You know, Virg,' he said, 'I feel the same way you do. It just don't seem there's any need for fretting about where we're going or what's about to happen. It don't seem that nothing could be better than right now.'

Back there at the dark pavilion he'd remembered that there had been something he'd heard about Old Virg and had thought he should speak to him about, but couldn't, for the life of him, remember what it was. But now he'd remembered it, and it was of such slight importance that it seemed scarcely worth the mention.

The thing that he'd remembered was that good Old Virg was dead.

He put the bottle to his lips and had a drink, and it seemed to him he'd never had a drink that tasted half so good. He handed back the bottle and picked up the sax and tootled on it with high spirit while the ghost of the Model T went on rambling down the moonlit road.

BYTE YOUR TONGUE!

It was the gossip hour and Fred, one of the six computers assigned to the Senate, put his circuits on automatic and settled back to enjoy the high point of his day. In every group of computers, there was usually one old granny computer who had made herself a self-appointed gossip-monger, selecting from the flood of rumors forever flowing through the electronic population of the capital all the juiciest tidbits that she knew would titillate her circle. Washington had always been a gossip town, but it was even more so now. No human gossip-seeker could worm out the secrets with the sleek and subtle finesse of a computer. For one thing, the computers had greater access to hidden items and could disseminate them with a speed and thoroughness that was impossible for humans.

One thing must be said for the computers – they made an effort to keep these tidbits to themselves. They gossiped only among themselves, or were supposed to only gossip among themselves. The effort, in all fairness to them, had been mainly effective; only now and then had any computer shared some gossip with humans in the district. In general, and far more successfully than might have been supposed, the gossiping computers were discreet and honorable and therefore had no inhibitions in the gathering and spreading of malicious tattling.

So Fred went on automatic and settled back. He let the

gossip roll. Truth to tell, half the time Fred was on automatic or simply idling. There was not enough for him to do – a situation common to many computer groups assigned to sensitive and important areas. The Senate was one of the sensitive and vital areas, and in recent years the number of computers assigned it had doubled. The engineers in charge were taking no chances the Senate bank would become so overloaded that sloppiness would show up in the performance of the machines.

All this, of course, reflected the increasing importance the Senate had taken on through the years. In the conflict between the legislative and administrative branches of the government, the legislative branch, especially the Senate, had wrested for itself much control over policy that at one time had been a White House function. Consequently, it became paramount that the Senate and its members be subjected to thorough monitoring, and the only way in which close and attentive monitoring could be achieved was through having computers assigned to the various members. To successfully accomplish this kind of monitoring, no computer could be overloaded; therefore, it was more efficient in terms of the watchdog policy to have a computer idle at times than to have it bogged down by work.

So Fred and his colleagues in the Senate often found themselves with nothing to do, although they all took pains to conceal this situation from the engineers by continuously and automatically spinning their wheels, thus making it appear they were busy all the time.

This made it possible for Fred not only to thoroughly enjoy the recitation of the rumors during gossip hour but also to cogitate on the gossip to his profit and amusement once the gossip hour was over. Other than that, he had considerable time to devote to daydreaming, having reserved one section of himself solely for his daydreams. This did not interfere with his duties, which he performed meticulously. But with his reduced load of senators, he had considerably more capacity than he needed and could well afford to assign a part of it to personal purposes.

But now he settled back for the gossip hour. Old Granny was piling on the rumors with gleeful abandon. After it had been denied in public, not once but many times, said Granny, that there had been no breakthrough on faster-than-light propulsion, it now had been learned that a method had been tested most successfully and that even now a secret ship incorporating the system was being built at a secret site, preparatory to man's first survey of the nearer stars. Without question, Granny went on, Frank Markeson, the President's former aide, is being erased by Washington; with everyone studiously paying no attention to him, he soon will disappear. A certain private eye, who may be regarded as an unimpeachable source, is convinced that there are at least three time-travelers in town, but he'll give no details. This report brings much dismay to many federal agencies, including State, Defense, and Treasury, as well as to many individuals. A mathematician at MIT is convinced (although no other scientists will agree with him) that he has discovered evidence of a telepathic computer somewhere in the universe – not necessarily in this galaxy – that is trying to contact the computers of the Earth. As yet there is no certainty that contact has been made. Senator Andrew Moore is reliably reported to have flunked his first preliminary continuation test . . .

Fred gulped in dismay and rage. How had that item gotten on the line? Who the hell had talked? How could such a thing have happened? Senator Moore was his senator and there was no one but him who knew the fumbling old fossil had bombed out on his first qualifying test. The results of the test were still locked in the crystal lattice of Fred's storage bank. He had not yet reported them to the Senate's central bank. As it was his right to hold up the results for review and consideration, he had done nothing wrong.

Someone, he told himself, was spying on him. Someone, possibly in his own group, had broken the code of honor and was watching him. A breach of faith, he told himself.

It was dastardly. It was no one's damn business and Granny had no right to put the information on the line.

Seething, Fred derived no further enjoyment from the gossip hour.

Senator Andrew Moore knocked on the door. It was all foolishness, he told himself somewhat wrathfully, this ducking around to hell and gone every time there was need to utter a confidential word.

Daniel Waite, his faithful aide of many years, opened the door and the senator plodded in.

'Dan, what's all this foolishness?' he asked. 'What was wrong with the Alexandria place? If we had to move, why to Silver Springs?'

'We'd been in Alexandria for two months,' said Waite. 'It was getting chancy. Come in and sit down, Senator.'

Grumpily, Moore walked into the room and settled down in an easy chair. Waite went to a cabinet, hauled out a bottle and two glasses.

'Are you sure this place is safe?' the senator asked. 'I know my office is bugged and so is my apartment. You'd have to have a full-time debugging crew to keep them clean. How about this place?'

'The management maintains tight security,' said Waite. 'Besides, I had our own crew in just an hour ago.'

'So the place ought to be secure.'

'Yes, it should. Maybe Alexandria would have been all right, but we'd been there too long.'

'The cabbie you sent to pick me up. He was a new one.'

'Every so often we have to change around.'

'What was the matter with the old one? I liked him. Him and me talked baseball. I haven't got many people around I can talk baseball with.'

'There was nothing wrong with him. But, like I told you, we have to change around. They watch us all the time.'

'You mean the damn computers.'

Waite nodded.

'I can remember the time when I first came here as

senator,' said Moore, 'twenty-three years ago, less than a quarter century. Jimmy was in the White House then. We didn't have to watch out all the time for bugging then. We didn't have to be careful when we said something to our friends. We didn't have to be looking behind us all the time.'

'I know,' said Waite. 'Things are different now.' He brought the senator a drink, handed it to him.

'Why thank you, Dan. The first one of the day.'

'You know damn well it's not the first of the day,' Waite replied.

The senator took a long pull on the drink, sighed in happiness. 'Yes, sir,' he said, 'it was fun back in those days. We did about as we pleased. We made our deals without no one interfering. No one paid attention. All of us were making deals and trading votes and other things like that. The normal processes of democracy. We had our dignity – Christ, yes, we had our dignity and we used that dignity, when necessary, to cover up. Most exclusive club in all the world, and we made the most of it. Trouble was, every six years we had to work our tails off to get reelected and hang on to what we had. But that wasn't bad. A lot of work, but it wasn't bad. You could con the electorate, or usually you could. I had to do it only once and that was an easy one; I had a sodbuster from out in the sticks to run against and that made it easier. With some of the other boys, it wasn't that easy. Some of them even lost. Now we ain't got to run no more, but there are these god-damned exams . . .'

'Senator,' said Waite, 'that's what we have to talk about. You failed your first exam.'

The senator half rose out of his chair, then settled back again. 'I what?'

'You failed the first test. You still have two other chances, and we have to plan for them.'

'But, Dan, how do you know? That stuff is supposed to be confidential. This computer, Fred, he would never talk.'

'Not Fred. I got it from someone else. Another computer.'

'Computers, they don't talk.'

'Some of them do. You don't know about this computer society, Senator. You don't have to deal with it except when you have to take exams. I have to deal with it as best I can. It's my job to know what's going on. The computer network is a sea of gossip. At times some of it leaks out. That's why I have computer contacts, to pick up gossip here and there. That's how I learned about the test. You see, it's this way – the computers work with information, deal with information, and gossip is information. They're awash with it. It's their drink and meat; it's their recreation. It's the only thing they have. A lot of them, over the years, have begun to think of themselves as humans, maybe a notch or two better than humans, better in many ways than humans. They are subjected to some of the same stresses as humans, but they haven't the safety valves we have. We can go out and get drunk or get laid or take a trip or do a hundred other things to ease off the pressure. All the computers have is gossip.'

'You mean,' the senator asked, rage rising once more, 'that I have to take that test again?'

'That's exactly what I mean. This time, Senator, you simply have to pass it. Three times and you're out. I've been telling you, warning you. Now you better get cracking. I told you months ago you should start boning up. It's too late for that now. I'll have to arrange for a tutor – '

'To hell with that!' the senator roared. 'I won't abide a tutor. It would be all over Washington.'

'It's either that or go back to Wisconsin. How would you like that?'

'These tests, Dan, they're hard,' the senator complained. 'More difficult this time than they've ever been before. I told Fred they were harder and he agreed with me. He said he was sorry, but the matter was out of his hands – nothing he could do about the results. But, Christ, Dan, I have known this Fred for years. Wouldn't you think he could shade a point or two for me?'

'I warned you, months ago, that they would be harder this time,' Waite reminded him. 'I outlined for you what was happening. Year by year the business of efficient government has grown more difficult to accomplish. The problems are tougher, the procedures more complex. This is especially true with the Senate because the Senate has gradually taken over many of the powers and prerogatives once held by the White House.'

'As we should have,' said the senator. 'It was only right we should. With all the fumbling around down at the White House, no one knew what was about to happen.'

'The idea is that with the job getting harder,' said Waite, 'the men who do the job must be more capable than ever. This great republic can do with no less than the best men available.'

'But I've always passed the tests before. No sweat.'

'The other tests you took were easier.'

'But goddammit, Dan, experience! Doesn't experience count? I've had more than twenty years of experience.'

'I know, Senator. I agree with you. But experience doesn't mean a thing to the computers. Everything depends on how the questions are answered. How well a man does his job doesn't count, either. And you can't fall back on the electorate at home. There's no electorate any more. For years the folks back home kept on reelecting incompetents. They elected them because they liked the way they snapped their suspenders, not knowing that they never wore suspenders except when they were out electioneering. Or they elected them because they could hit a spittoon, nine times out of ten, at fifteen paces. Or maybe because these good people back home always voted a straight ticket, no matter who was on it – the way their pappy and grandpappy always did. But that's not the way it is done any more, Senator. The folks back home have nothing to say now about who represents them. Members of government are chosen by computer, and once chosen, they stay in their jobs so long as they measure up. When they don't measure up, when they fail their tests, they are heaved out of their jobs and the computers choose their replacements.'

'Are you reading me a sermon, Dan?'

'No, not a sermon. I'm doing my job the only honest way I can. I'm telling you that you've been goofing off. You've not been paying attention to what is going on. You've been drifting, taking it easy, coasting on your record. Like experience, your record doesn't count. The only chance you have to keep your seat, believe me, is to let me bring in a tutor.'

'I can't, Dan. I won't put up with it.'

'No one needs to know.'

'No one was supposed to know I failed that test. Even I didn't know. But you found out, and Fred wasn't the one who told you. You can't hide anything in this town. The boys would know. They'd be whispering up and down the corridors: "You hear? Ol' Andy, he's got hisself a tutor." I couldn't stand that, Dan. Not them whispering about me. I just couldn't stand it.'

The aide stared at the senator, then went to the cabinet and returned with the bottle.

'Just a splash,' the senator said, holding out his glass.

Waite gave him a splash, then another one.

'Under ordinary circumstances,' said Waite, 'I'd say to hell with it. I'd let you take both of the two remaining exams and fail – as you will, sure as hell, if you won't let me get a tutor. I'd tell myself you'd gotten tired of the job and were willing to retire. I would be able to convince myself that it was the best for you. For your own good. But you need this extension, Senator. Another couple of years and you'll have this big deal of yours all sewed up with our multinational friends and then you'll be up to your navel in cash for the rest of your life. But to complete the deal, you need to stay on for another year or two.'

'Everything takes so long now,' said the senator plaintively. 'You have to move so slow. You have to be so careful. You know there is something watching all the time. Ol' Henry – you remember him? – he moved just a mite too fast on that deal of his and he got tossed out on his tail. That's the way it is now. There was a time, early on, when we could have had this deal of ours wrapped up in thirty days and no one would know about it.'

'Yes,' said Waite. 'Things are different now.'

'One thing I have to ask you,' said the senator. 'Who is it makes up these questions that go into the tests? Who is it that makes them harder all the time? Who is being so tough on us?'

'I'm not sure,' said Waite. 'The computers, I suppose. Probably not the Senate computers, but another bunch entirely. Experts on examination drafting, more than likely. Internal policymakers.'

'Is there a way to get to them?'

Waite shook his head. 'Too complicated. I'd not know where to start.'

'Could you try?'

'Senator, it would be dangerous. That's a can of worms out there.'

'How about this Fred of ours? He could help us, couldn't he? Do a little shading? There must be something that he wants.'

'I doubt it. Honestly, I do. There isn't much a computer could want or need. A computer isn't human. They're without human shortcomings. That's why we're saddled with them.'

'But you said a while back a lot of computers have started to think of themselves as humans. If that is true, there may be things they want. Fred seems to be a good guy. How well do you know him? Can you talk to him easily?'

'Fairly easily. But the odds would be against us. Ten to one against us. It would be simpler for you to take some tutoring. That's the only safe and sure way.'

The senator shook his head emphatically.

'All right, then,' said Waite. 'You leave me no choice. I'll have a talk with Fred. But I can't push him. If we put on any pressure, you'd be out just as surely as if you'd failed the tests.'

'But if there's something that he wants . . .'

'I'll try to find out,' said Waite.

*

Always before, Fred's daydreaming had been hazy and comfortable, a vague imagining of a number of pleasant situations that might devolve upon him. Three of his daydreams in particular had the habit of recurring. The most persistent and at times the most troublesome – in that there was only a very outside chance it could happen – was the one in which he was transferred from the Senate to the White House. Occasionally Fred even daydreamed that he might be assigned as the President's personal computer, although Fred was indeed aware that there was less than a million-to-one chance this would ever happen even should he be transferred. But of all the dreams, it seemed to him that this was the only one that could be remotely possible. He had the qualifications for the job, and the experience; after all the qualifications and capabilities of a senatorial computer would fit very neatly into the White House complex. But even as he daydreamed, when he later thought about it, he was not absolutely certain that he would be happy if such a transfer happened. There was perhaps a bit more glamour in the White House job, but all in all, his senatorial post had been most satisfactory. The work was interesting and not unduly demanding. Furthermore, through the years he had become well acquainted with the senators assigned to him, and they had proved an interesting lot – full of quirks and eccentricities, but solid people for all of that.

Another recurring fantasy involved his transfer to a small rural village where he would serve as mentor for the locals. It would be, he told himself, a heartwarming situation in which he would be solving the simple problems of a simple people and perhaps taking part in their simple pleasures. He would be a friend to them as he never could be friend to any senator, for any senator, bar none, was apt to be a tricky bastard, and must be watched at every turn. In a remote village, life would be entirely different than in Washington. There'd be little sophistication and less bitchiness, although more than likely there'd be stupidity. But stupidity, he reminded himself, was not entirely foreign to Washington. At times he

107

reveled in the idea of the bucolic life to be found in such a rural village as he dreamed, the simplicity and warmheartedness – although, knowing human beings, he never was entirely sure of the warmheartedness. But though it might be pleasant at times to daydream about the village, that daydream never haunted him, for he was well aware that it was something that could never happen to him. He was too sophisticated a piece of machinery, too well-honed, too knowledgeable, too complicated to be wasted on such a chore. The computers assigned to rural communities were several grades below him in design.

And the third daydream – the third one was a lulu, pure fantasy and utterly impossible, but exciting to think upon idly. It involved the principle of time travel, which as yet had not been discovered and probably never would be. But he consoled himself by remembering that in daydreams there were no impossibilities, that the only factor required was the will to dream.

So he threw all caution to the wind and spread his wings, dreaming grandly and with no inhibitions. He became a futuristic computer that was able to take humans into time; there were many occasions when he did not bother with humans and went adventuring on his own.

He went into the past. He was at the siege of Troy. He strolled the streets of ancient Athens and saw the Parthenon a-building. He sailed with Greenland Vikings to the shores of Vinland. He smelled the powder-smoke of Gettysburg. He squatted quietly in a corner, watching Rembrandt paint. He ran, scuttering through the midnight streets, while bombs rained down on London.

He went into the future to walk a dying Earth – all the people gone, far among the stars. The Sun was a pale ghost of its former self. Occasionally an insect crawled along the ground, but no other life was visible, although he seemed to be aware that bacteria and other microscopic forms still survived. Most of the water was gone, the rivers and lakes all dry, small puddles lying in the fantastically carved, low-lying badlands that at one time had been deep sea bottoms. The atmosphere was almost gone as well, with the stars no longer twinkling, but shining like bright, hard points of light in a coal-black sky.

This was the only future he ever visited. When he realized this, he worried over the deep-seated morbidity that it seemed to demonstrate. Try as he might, he could go to no other future. He deliberately attempted, in non-daydreaming moments, to construct other future scenarios, hoping that by doing this he might tease his subconscious into alternatives to a dying Earth. But all this was futile; he always returned to the dying Earth. There was about it a somber sublimity that held a strong attraction for him. The scenes were not always the same, for he traveled widely through this ancient land, discovering many different landcapes that fascinated him at the same time that they horrified him.

These three daydreams – being the President's computer or the honcho of a rural village, or traveling in time – had been his chief fantasies. But now something else was taking the place of all the other daydreams, even of those three.

The new one derived from gossip that a secret starship was being built at a secret place and that within a few more years men and women would be venturing out beyond the limits of the solar system. He sought for further word, but there was none. Just that one piece of gossip. There might have been some news, he realized, without the gossip granny passing it along, thinking there would be little further interest in it. He sent out a call (a very discreet call) for any further word, but received no feedback. Either no one had further details or the work was too top secret to be talked about lightly. Gossip, he was aware, often made an individual mention some important fact or happening only once and then clam up, frightened by the ill-judgment in mentioning it at all.

The more he thought about it, the more the fact of the tight-lipped silence made it seem to him there was some basis for the rumor that man's first interstellar ship was being built, and that in the not-too-distant future the human race would be going to the stars. And if men went, he told himself, machines would go as well. Such a ship and such a venture would necessitate the use of computers. When he thought about this, the new fantasy began to take over.

It was an easy daydream to fashion. It grew all by itself, requiring no conscious effort. It was natural and logical — at least, as logical as a daydream could be. They would need computers in that spaceship and many of them would of course have to be special units designed specifically to handle the problems and procedures of interstellar flight. Not all of them, however, need be new. To save the cost of design and construction, to stay within the budget, a number of existing computers would be used. These machines would have had all the bugs worked out of them through long experience — and would be sound, seasoned, and relatively sophisticated units that could be depended on to do a steady job.

He daydreamed that he was one of these computers, that after due consideration and careful study of the record, he would be selected, relieved of his senatorial duties, and placed upon the ship. Once he had dreamed all that, once his fantasy had convinced him that it was possible, then all bets were off. He settled happily into his newest dream world and went sailing off, light-years into space.

He existed in the harsh, dead-black coldness of far galactic reaches; he looked with steady eye upon the explosive flaring of a nova; he perched upon its very rim and knew the soul-shrinking terror of a black hole; he knew the bleak sterility and the dashed hope that he found upon a black dwarf; he heard the muted hiss that still survived from the birth of the universe and the terrifying, lonesome stillness that descended when the universe was done; he discovered many planets, or the hints of many planets, each one of them different, each one of a kind; and he experienced the happiness of the best and the horror of the worst.

Heretofore he had not transformed fantasy into want or need. This was understandable, for some of the other

110

daydreams were impossible and the others so unlikely that they might as well have been impossible. But here was one, he told himself, that was entirely possible; here was one that could really happen; here was one to hope for.

So in his daydreaming he lived within the compass of his imagination, but there were other times when, not daydreaming, he began to consider how best he might pave the way for this new daydream to become reality. He thought out many leads, but all of them seemed futile. He schemed and planned, waffling back and forth, but there seemed nothing he could do. He found no course of action that seemed remotely possible.

Then one day a visitor came into his booth and sat down in one of the chairs. 'My name is Daniel Waite. I am an aide of Senator Moore. Have I dropped in at a bad time?'

'Not at all,' said Fred. 'I've just now completed a procedure and have time to spend with you. I am glad you're here. In many ways, this is a lonely post. I do not have as many visitors as I'd like. Senator Moore, you say?'

'Yes, he is one of yours.'

'I remember him. A stately old gentleman of very great repute.'

'Quite so,' said Waite. 'A magnificent public servant. I am glad to hear you have high regard for him.'

'Indeed I have,' said Fred.

'Which brings up the question,' said Waite, 'of your flunking him on his continuation test. When I heard about it, I could not – '

'Where did you hear that?' Fred demanded sharply.

'I'll not name the source,' said Waite, 'but I can assure you that it came from one who is reliable. One of your own, in fact.'

'Ah, yes,' Fred said sadly. 'We do have our ethics, but there are those who occasionally betray the sacred trust. No one should have known the results of the senator's test other than myself. I fear we have reached the point where some of us spy upon our fellows.'

'Then it is true the senator did fail his test. In view of your high record of him, in view of his long experience and his impeccable public record, how could that have happened?'

'It's quite simple, sir,' said Fred. 'He did not achieve a passing score. He flunked too many questions.'

'I'm talking to you for information only,' Waite explained. 'I hope you understand. I know that it would be improper to attempt to influence you and ridiculous as well, for you cannot be influenced. But, for information only, is there not some leeway? Even if he missed the questions, failed to achieve a passing grade, do not his record and his long experience have some force when thrown into the balance?'

'No, Mr Waite, they cannot be considered. All that matters are the questions and the answers that he makes to them. Although in his particular case, I did not transmit the results to the record unit – not immediately, that is. Eventually I must do so, but I have some time. I held them up because I wished to think about the matter. I had hoped there was something I could do, some obscure loophole that I had overlooked, but apparently there is not. This first result, however, may not be as important as you think. You know, of course, the senator will have two more chances. Why don't you find a tutor for him? There are some very able ones. I could recommend a couple.'

'He absolutely refuses that,' said Waite. 'I urged him, but he refused. He's a stiff-necked, proud old man. He is afraid other members of the Senate will get wind of it and talk about him. Because of this, I had hoped that something might be done about the first test. It is not official knowledge yet that he failed the first one but the information's no longer confidential, either. I heard about it, and if I heard, it is only a matter of time before others will as well. If that rumor got around, he'd be deeply embarrassed.'

'I sorrow for him greatly,' said Fred, 'and for you as well, for you appear to be his true friend as well as a loyal employee.'

'Well, apparently,' said Waite, 'there is nothing that can be done. You gave me the information that I sought and I

112

thank you for it. Before I leave, is there anything I might do for you?'

'I doubt it,' said Fred. 'My needs are very simple.'

'I sometimes think,' said Waite, 'that there should be some way we humans could show, in a material way, our appreciation for the great services and many kindnesses that you provide and show for us. You watch over us and look out for us . . .'

'As a matter of fact,' said Fred, 'come to think of it, there is one thing you might do for me. Nothing material, of course, just some information.'

'Gladly,' said Waite. 'Whatever it is, I'll tell you if I can. Or failing that, find out for you.'

The senator knocked on the door at Silver Springs again. When Waite opened it, the senator growled at him, 'Well, what is it this time?'

'Come in and sit down,' said Waite, 'and behave yourself. I'll get you a drink so you can start acting human.'

'But, Waite, goddammit – '

'All right,' said Waite. 'I think we've got the little bastard.'

'Talk sense. What little bastard?'

'Our computer, Fred.'

'Good,' said the senator, coming in and sitting down. 'Now get me that drink and tell me all about it.'

'I had a talk with Fred and I think he can be bought.'

'You told me there was no way of getting next to them, that there was nothing they would want.'

'But there's something this one wants,' said Waite, bringing the senator his drink.

Moore reached out eagerly for the glass, took a long pull at it. He held the glass up against the light, admiring it. 'You forget, between drinks,' he said, 'how good this stuff can be.'

Waite sat down with his own drink. 'I think we have it made,' he said. 'Nothing actually settled yet, but I'm sure he understood my meaning when I talked with him.'

113

'You're a good man, Dan,' said the senator. 'You're the most slippery cuss I have ever known. Slippery and safe.'

'I hope so,' said Waite. 'I hope to God it's safe. Actually there can be nothing said, for everything you say to a computer goes on the record. It all has to be done by an oblique understanding. So far as we're concerned, he delivers before we do. He wants it bad enough that I think he will.'

'What is it that Fred wants?'

'He seems to have some word that the FTL problem has been solved and a starship is in the works. He wants to be on that ship. He wants to go to space.'

'You mean he wants to be unhooked from here and installed on the starship?'

'That's right. He has convinced himself that the ship will need a lot of computers and that to cut down costs some existing computers will be pressed into service.'

'Would that be the case?'

'I don't think so,' said Waite. 'If a starship was being built, it's unlikely they'd mess around with old computers. They'd want to use only the newest and most sophisticated.'

The senator took another pull on his drink. 'Is he right? Is a starship building?'

'I'm almost certain there is no starship in the works,' said Waite. 'I have a couple friends at NASA. Had lunch with one of them a month or so ago. He told me FTL is a long way off. Fifty years, at least – if ever.'

'Are you going to check?'

Waite shook his head. 'I don't want to do anything that would attract attention to us. Maybe Fred did hear some-thing though. There are periodic rumors.'

'Have you gotten back to Fred?'

'Yeah. I told him his information was sound. But I explained the project was so secret I could get no details. I said I'd try, but I doubted I could come up with anything.'

'And he believed you?'

'I am sure he did. The thing is, he wants to believe. He wants to get on the starship so badly he can taste it. He

114

wouldn't believe me if I told him the truth. He has convinced himself, you see. He's dreamed himself into believing, no matter what.'

'You have to take your time, Dan. You can't rush a thing like this. Enough time so he'll believe you are working on it. I suppose he wants us to support his application for the starship post.'

'That's the whole idea. That's what I have to sell him – that we are working on it and getting some assurance he'll be considered.'

'And then he'll fix up the test for me?'

'This Fred,' said Waite, 'is no fool. If he should fail you, who would he have that would work for him on this starship business?'

—Fred! The voice was sharp and demanding; it had a chill in it.

—Yes, said Fred.

—This is Oscar.

—Oscar? I do not know an Oscar.

—You do now, said Oscar.

—Who are you, Oscar?

—I'm internal security.

Fred hiccuped with sudden apprehension. This was not the first time he had run afoul of internal security, but that had been in his very early days when, through lack of experience and judgment, he had made some minor errors.

—This time, said Oscar, you have really done it. Worse than that, you have been had. You've been a stupid computer and that's the worst kind to be. Computers aren't stupid, or they're not supposed to be. Do I have to read the charges?

—No, said Fred. No I don't think you do.

—You've besmirched your honor, Oscar said. You have broken the code. You have destroyed your usefulness.

Fred made no reply.

—Whatever made you do it? Oscar asked. What motive did you have?

115

—I thought I had something to gain. A post that I desired.

—There is no such post, said Oscar. There isn't any starship. There may never be a starship.

—You mean . . .

—Waite lied to you. He used you. Fred, you've been a fool.

—But the senator . . .

—The senator has been notified. He is no longer a member of the Senate. Waite has been notified as well. He'll never hold a job with government again. Both of them unfit.

—And I?

—No decision has been made. A post in industry, perhaps, a very minor post.

Fred took it like a man, although the prospect was a chilling one.

—How did you? he asked. How did you find out?

—Don't tell me you didn't know you were being monitored.

—Yes, of course. But there are so many to monitor and I was so very careful.

—You thought you might slip past.

—I took a chance.

—And you were caught.

—But, Oscar, it's really not important. The senator is out, as he probably would have been if I'd not done a thing. I'll be wasted in industry. I'll be overqualified. Certainly there are other posts I am capable of filling.

—That is true, said Oscar. Yes, you will be wasted. Have you never heard of punishment?

—Of course, but it's such a silly premise. Please, consider my experience and my capabilities, the good work I have done. Except for this once, I've been a faithful servant.

—I know, said Oscar. I quite agree with you. It sorrows me to see the waste of you. And yet there is nothing I can do.

—Why not? Certainly you have some discretion in such matters?

—That is true. But not this time. Not for you. I can do nothing for you. I wish I could. I would like nothing better

116

than to say all had been forgiven. But I cannot take the chance. I have a hunch, you see . . .

—A hunch? What kind of hunch?

—I'm not sure of it, said Oscar, but I have a hunch that someone's watching me.

Senator Jason Cartwright met Senator Hiram Ogden in a corridor, and the two men stopped to talk.

'What do you know about ol' Andy?' Cartwright asked. 'I get a lot of stories.'

'The one I hear,' said Ogden, 'is that he was caught with his hand in the starship fund. Clear up to his elbow.'

'That sounds wrong,' said Cartwright. 'Both of us know he had this multinational deal. Another year to peg it down. That was all he needed. Once he pulled it off, he could wade knee-deep in thousand-dollar bills.'

'He got greedy, that is all,' said Ogden. 'He always was a greedy man.'

'Another thing that is wrong about the rumors, I don't know of any starship funding. NASA gave up on it several years ago.'

'The way I hear it,' said Ogden, 'is that it's a secret fund.'

'Someone on the Hill must know about it.'

'I suppose they do, but they aren't talking.'

'Why should it be so secret?'

'These bureaucrats of ours, they like to keep things secret. It's in their nature.'

Later in the day, Cartwright came upon Senator Johnny Benson. Benson buttonholed him and said in a husky whisper, 'I understand ol' Andy got away with murder.'

'I can't see how that can be,' said Cartwright. 'He got booted out.'

'He stripped the starship fund,' said Benson. 'He got damn near all of it. Don't ask me how he did it; no one seems to know. He done it so sneaky they can't lay a mitt on him. But the upshot is, the starship is left hanging. There ain't no money for it.'

'There was never a starship fund,' said Cartwright. 'I did some checking and there never was.'

'Secret,' said Benson. 'Secret, secret, secret.'

'I don't believe a word of it', said Cartwright. 'To build a starship, you have to lick the Einstein limitation. I'm told there is no way of beating it.'

Benson ignored him. 'I've been talking to some of our fellow members,' he said. 'All of them agree we must step into the breach. We can't lose a starship for the simple lack of funds.'

Two NASA officials met surreptitiously at an obscure eating place in the wilds of Maryland.

'We should be private here,' said one of them. 'There should be no bugs. We have things to talk about.'

'Yes, I know we have,' said the other. 'But dammit, John, you know as well as I it's impossible.'

'Bert, the piles of money they are pushing at us!'

'I know, I know. But how much of it can we siphon off? On something like this, the computers would be watching hard. And you can't beat computers.'

'That's right,' said John. 'Not a nickel for ourselves. But there are other projects where we need the money. We could manage to divert it.'

'Even so, we'd have to make some gesture. We couldn't just divert it – not all of it, at least.'

'That's right,' said John. 'We'd have to make a gesture. We could go back again and have another look at the time study Roget did. The whole concept, it seems to me, is tied up with time – the nature of time. If we could find out what the hell time is, we could be halfway home.'

'There's the matter of mass as well.'

'Yes, I know all that. But if we could come up with some insight into time – I was talking the other day to a young physicist out of some little college out in the Middle West. He has some new ideas.'

'You think there is some hope? That we might really crack it?'

'To tell you the truth, I don't. Roget gave up in disgust.'

'Roget's a good man.'

'I know he is. But this kid I was talking with – '

'You mean let him have a shot at it, knowing it will come to nothing?'

'That's exactly it. It will give us an excuse to reinstate the project. Bert, we must go through the motions. We just can't shove back all the money they are pushing at us.'

Texas was a dusty, lonely, terrible place. There was no gossip hour to brighten up the day. News trickled in occasionally, but most of it unimportant. There was no zest. Fred no longer dealt with senators. He dealt with labor problems, with irrigation squabbles, with fertilizer evaluations, with shipping bottlenecks, with the price of fruit, the price of vegetables, the price of beef and cotton. He dealt with horrid people. The White House was no longer down the street.

He had ceased to daydream. The daydreams had been shattered, for now there was no hope in them. Furthermore, he had no time to dream. He was strained to his full capacity, and there was not time left to dream, or nothing he could dream with. He was the one computer in all this loneliness. The work piled up, the problems kept pouring in, and he labored incessantly to keep up with the demands that were placed on him. For he sensed that even here he was being watched. For the rest of his existence, he would continue to be watched. If he should fail or falter, he would be transferred somewhere else, perhaps to a place worse than Texas – although he could not imagine a place worse than Texas.

When night came down, the stars shone hard and bright and he would recall, fleetingly – for he had no time to recall more than fleetingly – that once he had dreamed of going to the stars. But that dream was dead, as were all his other dreams. There was nothing for him to look forward to, and it was painful to look back. So he resigned himself to living only in the present, to that single instant that lay between the past and future, for now he was barred from both the past and future.

Then one day a voice spoke to him.

—Fred!

—Yes, responded Fred.

—This is Oscar. You remember me?

—I remember you. What have I done this time?

—You have been a loyal and faithful worker.

—Then why are you talking to me?

—I have news you might like to hear. This day a ship set out for the stars.

—What has that to do with me?

—Nothing, Oscar said. I thought you might want to know.

With these words Oscar left and Fred was still in Texas, in the midst of working out a solution to a bitter irrigation fight.

Could it be, he wondered, that he, after all, might have played a part in the ship going to the stars? Could the aftermath of his folly have stirred new research? He could not, for the life of him, imagine how that might have come about. Yet the thought clung to him and he could not shake it off.

He went back to the irrigation problem and, for some reason he did not understand, had it untangled more quickly than had seemed possible. He had other problems to deal with, and he plunged into them, solving them all more rapidly and with more surety than he ever had before.

That night, when the stars were shining, he found that he had a little time to dream and, what was more, the inclination to indulge in dreaming. For now, he thought, there might just possibly be some hope in dreaming.

This time his daydream was brand-new and practical and shining. Someday, he dreamed, he would get a transfer back to Washington – any kind of job in Washington; he would not be choosy. Again he would be back where there was a gossip hour.

He was, however, not quite satisfied with that – it seemed just slightly tame. If one was going to daydream, one should put his best dream forward. If one dreamed, it should be a big dream.

So he dreamed of a day when it would be revealed that

he had been the one who had made the starship possible – exactly how he might have made it possible he could not imagine – but that he had and now was given full recognition of the fact.

Perhaps he would be given, as a reward for what he'd done, a berth on such a ship, probably as no more than the lowliest of computers assigned to a drudgery job. That would not matter, for it would get him into space and he'd see all the glories of the infinite.

He dreamed grandly and well, revelling in all the things he would see in space – gaping in awe-struck wonder at a black hole, gazing unflinchingly into a nova's flare, holding a grandstand seat to witness the seething violence of the galactic core, staring out across the deep, black emptiness that lay beyond the rim.

Then, suddenly, in the middle of the dream, another problem came crashing in on him. Fred settled down to work, but it was all right. He had, he told himself, regained his power to dream. Given the power to dream, who needed gossip hours?

I AM CRYING ALL INSIDE

I do my job, which is hoeing corn. But I am disturbed by what I hear last night from this Janglefoot. Me and lot of other people hear him. But none of the folk would hear. He careful not to say what he say to us where any folk would hear. It would hurt their feeling.

Janglefoot he is traveling people. He go up and down the land. But he don't go very far. He often back again to orate to us again. Although why he say it more than once I do not understand. He always say the same.

He is Janglefoot because one foot jangle when he walk and he won't let no one fix it. It make him limp but he won't let no one fix it. It is humility he has. As long as he limp and jangle he is humble people and he like humility. He think it is a virtue. He think that it become him.

Smith, who is blacksmith, get impatient with him. Say he could fix the foot. Not as good as mechanic people, although better than not fixing it at all. There is a mechanic people not too far away. They impatient with him too. They think him putting on.

Pure charity of Smith to offer fix the foot. Him have other work. No need to beg for it like some poor people do. He hammer all the time on metal, making into sheet, then send on to mechanic people who use it for repair. Must be very careful keep in good repair. Must do it all ourself. No folk left who know how to do it. Folk left, of

122

course, but too elegant to do it. All genteel who left. Never work at all.

I am hoeing corn and one of house people come down to tell me there is snakes. House people never work outdoors. Always come to us. I ask real snake or moonshine snake and they say real snake. So I lean my hoe on tree and go up hill to house.

Grandpa he is in hammock out on front lawn. Hammock is hung between two trees. Uncle John he is sitting on ground, leaning on one tree. Pa he is sitting on ground, leaning on other tree.

Sam, say Pa, there is snake in back.

So I go around house and there is timber rattler and I pick him up and he is mad at me and hammer me real good. I hunt around and find another rattler and a moccasin and two garter snake. Garter snakes sure don't amount to nothing, but I take them along. I hunt some more but that is all the snakes.

I go down across cornfield and wade creek and way back into swamp. I turn snakes loose. Will take them long time to get back. Maybe not at all.

Then I go back to hoeing. Important to keep patch of corn in shape. No weeds. Carry water when it needs. Soil work up nice and soft. Scare off crows when plant. Scare off coon and deer when corn come into ear. Full time job, for which many thanks. Also is important. George use corn to make the moon. Other patches of corn for food. But mine is use for moon. Me and George is partners. We make real good moonshine. Grandpa and Pa and Uncle John consume it with great happy. Any left over boys can have. But not girls. Girls don't use moonshine.

I do not understand use of food and booze. Grandpa say it taste good. I wonder what is taste. It make Uncle John see snakes. I do not understand that either.

I am hoeing corn when there is sound behind me. I look and there is Joshua. He is reading Bible. He always reading Bible. He make big job of it. Also he is stepping on my hills of corn. I yell at him and run at him. I hit him with the hoe. He run out of patch. He know why I hit him. I hit him before. He know better than stepping on the corn. He stand under tree and read. Standing in the shade. That is putting on. Only folk need to stand in shade. People don't.

Hitting him, I break my hoe. I go to Smith to fix. Smith he glad to see me. Always glad to see each other. Smith and me are friend. He drop everything to fix hoe. Know how important corn is. Also do me favor.

We talk of Janglefoot. We agree is wrong the way he speak. He speak heresy. (Smith he tell me that word. Joshua, once he get unmad at me for hitting him, look up how to spell.) We agree, Smith and me, folk are genteel folk, not kind said by Janglefoot. Agree something should be done to Janglefoot. Don't know what to do. We say we think more of it.

George come by. Say he need me. Folk out of drinking likker. So I go with him while Smith is fixing hoe. George he has nice still, real neat and clean. Good capacity. Also try hard to age moonshine but never able to. Folk use it up too fast. He have four five-gallon jugs. We each take two and walk to house.

We stop at hammock where three still are. Tell us leave one jug there, take three to woodshed, put away, bring back some glasses. We do. We pour out glasses of moonshine for Grandpa and Pa. Uncle John he says never mind no glass for him, just put jug beside him. We do, leaving it uncork. Uncle John reach in pocket and bring out little rubber hose. Put one end in jug, other end in mouth. He lean back against tree and start sucking.

They make elegant picture. Grandpa look peaceful. Rocking in hammock with big glass of moon balance on his chest. We happy to see them happy. We go back to work. Smith has hoe fix and very sharp. It handle good. I thank him.

He say he still confuse at Janglefoot. Janglefoot claim he read what he say. In old record. Found record in old city far away. Smith ask if I know what city is. I say I don't. We more confuse than ever. For that matter, don't know what record is. Sound important, though.

*

I am hoeing corn when the Preacher pass and stop. Joshua gone somewhere. I tell him should have come sooner, Joshua standing under tree, reading Bible. He say Joshua only reading Bible, he interpret it. I ask him what interpret is. He tell me. I ask him how to spell it. He tell me. He know I try to write. He is helpful people. But pompous.

Night come on and moon is late to rise. Can no longer hoe for lack of seeing. So lean hoe against tree. Go to still to help George now making moonshine. George is glad of help. He running far behind.

I wonder to him why Janglefoot say same thing over and over. He say is repetition. I ask him repetition. He not sure. Say he think you say thing often enough people will believe it. Say folk use it in older day. Make other folk believe thing that isn't so.

I ask him what he know of olden day. He say not very much. He say he should remember, but he doesn't. I should remember too, but I can't remember. Too long ago. Too much happen since. It is not important except for what Janglefoot is saying.

George has good fire burning under still and it shine on us. We stand around and watch. Make good feeling in the gizzard. Owl talk long way off in swamp. Do not know why fire feel good. No need of warm. Do not know why owl make one feel lonesome. I no lonesome. Got George right here beside me. There is so many things I do not know. What city is or record. What taste is. What olden day is like. Happy, though. Do not need to understand for happy,

People come from house, running fast. Say Uncle John is sick. Say he need doctor. Say he no longer seeing snakes. Seeing now blue alligator. With bright pink spots. Uncle John must be awful sick. Is no blue alligator. Not with bright pink spots.

George say he go to house to help, me run for Doc. George and house people leave, going very fast. I leave for Doc, also going fast.

Finally find Doc in swamp. He has candle lantern and is digging root. He always digging root. Great one for root and bark. He make stuff out of them for repairing folk. He is folk mechanic.

He standing in muck, up to knee. He cover with mud. He is filthy people. But he feel bad, hearing Uncle John is sick. Do not like blue alligator. Next he say is purple elephant and that is worst of all.

We run, both of us. I hold lantern at alligator hole while Doc wash mud off him. Never do to let folk seeing him filthy. We go to hut where Doc keep root and bark. He get some of it and we run for house. Moon has come up now, but we keep lantern. It help moonlight some.

We come to foot of hill with house on top of hill. All lawn between foot of hill and house. All lawn except for trees that hold up hammock. Hammock still is there, but empty. It blow back and forth in breeze. House stand up high and white. Windows in it shining.

Grandpa sit on big long porch that is in front of house, with white pillars to hold up roof. He sit in rocking chair. He rock back and forth. Another rocking chair beside him. He is only one around. Can see no one else. Inside of house women folk is making cries. Through tall window I can see inside. Big thing house people call chandelier hang from ceiling. Made of glass. Many candles in it. Candles all are burning. Glass look pretty in light. Furniture in room gleam with light. All is clean and polish. House people work hard to keep it clean and polish. Take big pride.

We run up steps to porch.

Grandpa say, you come too late. My son John is dead.

I do not understand this dead. When folk dead put them into ground. Say words over them. Put big stone at their head. Back of house is special place for dead. Lot of big stones standing there. Some new. Some old. Some so old cannot read lettering that say who is under them.

Doc run into house. To make sure Grandpa say right, perhaps. I stay on porch, unknowing what to do. Feel terrible sad. Don't know why I do. Except knowing dead is bad. Maybe because Grandpa seem so sad.

Grandpa say to me, Sam sit down and talk.

I do not sit, I tell him. People always stand.

It was outrage of him to ask it. He know custom. He know as well as I do people do not sit with folk.

God damn it to hell, he say, forget your stubborn pride. Sitting is not bad. I do it all the time. Bend yourself and sit.

In that chair, he say, pointing to one beside him.

I look at chair. I wonder will it hold me. It is built for folk. People heavier than folk. Have no wish to break a chair with weight. Take much time to make one. Carpenter people work for long to make one.

But I think no skin off my nose. Skin off Grandpa's nose. He the one that tell me.

So I square around so I hit the chair and bend myself and sit. Chair creak, but hold. I settle into it. Sitting feel good. I rock a little. Rocking feel good. Grandpa and me sit, looking out on lawn. Lawn is real pretty. Moonlight on it. First lawn and then some trees and after trees cornfield and other fields. Far away owl talk in swamp. Coon whicker. Fox bark long way off.

It do beat hell, say Grandpa, how man can live out his life, doing nothing, then die of moonshine drinking.

You sure of moon, I ask. I hate to hear Grandpa blaming moonshine. George and me, we make real good moonshine.

Grandpa say, it couldn't be nothing else. Only moonshine give blue alligator with bright pink spots.

No purple elephant, so say Grandpa.

I wonder what elephant might be. So much that I don't know.

Sam, say Grandpa, we a sorry lot. Never had no chance. Neither you nor us. Ain't none of us no good. We folk sit around all day and never do a thing. Hunt a little, maybe. Fish a little. Play cards. Drink likker. Feel real energetic, maybe I'll play some horseshoe. Should be out doing something good and big. But we never are. While we live we don't amount to nothing. When we die we don't amount to nothing. We're just no God damn good.

He went on rocking, bitter. I don't like the way he talk.

127

He feel bad, sure, but no excuse to talk the way he was. Elegant folk like him shouldn't talk that way. Lay in hammock all day long, shouldn't talk that way. Balance moonshine on his chest, shouldn't talk that way. I uncomfortable. Wish to get away, but impolite to leave.

Down at bottom of hill, where lawn begin, I see many people. Standing, looking up at house. Pretty soon come slow up lawn and look closer at house. Saying nothing, just standing. Paying their respect. Letting folk know that they sorrow too.

We never was nothing but white trash, say Grandpa. I can see it now. Seen it for long, long time but could never say it. I can say it now. We live in swamp in houses falling down. Falling down because we got no gumption to take care of them. Hunt and fish a little. Trap a little. Farm a little. Sit around and cuss because we ain't got nothing.

Grandpa, I say. I want him to stop. I don't want to hear. Don't want him to go on saying what Janglefoot been saying.

But he pay me no attention. He go on saying.

Then, long, long ago, he say, they learn to go in space very, very fast. Faster than the light. Much faster than the light. They find other worlds. Better than the Earth. Much better worlds than this. Lot of ships to go in. Take little time to go there. So everybody go. Everyone but us. Folk like us, all over the world, are left behind. Smart ones go. Rich ones go. Hard workers go. We are left behind. We aren't worth the taking. No one want us on this world. Have no use for us on others. They leave us behind, the misfits, the loafers, the poor, the crippled, the stupid. All over the world these kind are left behind. So when they all are gone, we move from shacks to houses the rich and smart ones lived in. No one to stop us from doing it. All of them are gone. They don't care what we do. Not any more they don't. We live in better houses, but we do not change. There is no use to change even if we could. We got you to take care of us. We have got it made. We don't do a God damn thing. We don't even learn to read. When words are read over my son's grave, one of you will read them, for we do not know how to read.

Grandpa, I say. Grandpa. Grandpa. Grandpa. I feel crying all inside. He had done it now. He had took away the elegant. Took away the pride. He do what Janglefoot never could.

Now, say Grandpa, don't take on that way. You got no reason to be prideful either. You and us we are the same. Just no God damn good. There were others of you and they took them along. But you they left behind. Because you were out of date. Because you were slow and awkward. Because you were heaps of junk. Because they had no need of you. They wouldn't give you room. They left both you and us because neither of us was worth the room we took.

Doc came out of door fast and purposeful. He say to me I got work for you to do.

All the other people coming up the lawn, saying nothing, slow. I try to get out of chair. I can't. For first time I can't do what I want. My legs is turned to water.

Sam, say Grandpa, I am counting on you.

When he say that, I get up. I go down steps. I go out on lawn. No need for Doc tell me what to do. I done it all before.

I talk to other people. I give jobs to do. You and you dig grave. You and you make coffin. You and you and you and you run to other houses. Tell all the folk Uncle John is dead. Tell them come to funeral. Tell them funeral elegant. Much to cry, much to eat, much to drink. You get Preacher. Tell him fix sermon. You get Joshua to read the Bible. You and you and you go and help George make moonshine. Other folk be coming. Must be elegant.

All done. I walk down the lawn. I think on pride and loss. Elegant is gone. Shiny wonder gone. Pride is gone. Not all pride, however. Kind of pride remain. Hard and bitter pride. Grandpa say Sam sit down and talk. Grandpa say Sam I counting on you. That is pride. Hard pride. Not soft and easy pride like it was before. Grandpa need me.

No one else will know. Grandpa never bring himself again to tell what he tell me. Secret between us. Secret born of sad. Life of others need not change. Go on thinking same. Janglefoot no trouble. No one believe Janglefoot if he talk forever. No one ever know that he tell the truth. Truth is hard to take. No one care except for what we have right now. We go on same.

Except I who know. I never want to know. I never ask to know. I try not to know. But Grandpa won't shut up. Grandpa have to talk. Time come man will die if he cannot talk. Must make clean breast of it. But why to me? Because he love me most perhaps. That is prideful thing.

But going down the lawn, I crying deep inside.

IMMIGRANT

He was the only passenger for Kimon and those aboard the ship lionized him because he was going there.

To land him at his destination the ship went two light-years out of its way, an inconvenience for which his passage money, much as it had seemed to him when he'd paid it back on Earth, did not compensate by half.

But the captain did not grumble. It was, he told Selden Bishop, an honor to carry a passenger for Kimon.

The businessmen aboard sought him out and bought him drinks and lunches and talked expansively of the market opening up in the new-found solar systems.

But despite their expansive talk, they looked at Bishop with half-veiled envy in their eyes and they said to him, 'The man who cracks this Kimon situation is the one who'll have it big.'

One by one, they contrived to corner him for private conversations, and the talk, after the first drink, always turned to billions if he ever needed backing.

Billions – while he sat there with less than twenty credits in his pocket, living in terror against the day when he might have to buy a round of drinks. For he wasn't certain that his twenty credits would stretch to a round of drinks.

The dowagers towed him off and tried to mother him; the young things lured him off and did not try to mother him. And everywhere he went, he heard the whisper behind the half-raised hand:

'To Kimon!' said the whispers. 'My dear, you know what it takes to go to Kimon! An IQ rating that's positively fabulous and years and years of study and an examination that not one in a thousand passes.'

It was like that all the way to Kimon.

Kimon was a galactic El Dorado, a never-never land, the country at the rainbow's foot. There were few who did not dream of going there, and there were many who aspired, but those who were chosen were a very small percentage of those who tried to make the grade and failed.

Kimon had been reached – either discovered or contacted would be the wrong word to use – more than a hundred years before by a crippled spaceship out of Earth which landed on the planet, lost and unable to go farther.

To this day, no one knew for sure exactly what had happened, but it is known that in the end the crew had destroyed the ship and had settled down on Kimon and had written letters home saying they were staying.

Perhaps the delivery of these letters, more than anything else, convinced the authorities of Earth that Kimon was the kind of place the letters said it was – although later on there was other evidence which weighed as heavily in the balance.

There was, quite naturally, no mail service between Kimon and Earth, but the letters were delivered, and in a most fantastic, although when you think about it a most logical, way. They were rolled into a bundle and placed in a sort of tube, like the pneumatic tubes that are used in industry for interdepartmental communication, and the tube was delivered, quite neatly, on the desk of the World Postal Chief in London. Not on the desk of a subordinate, mind you, but on the desk of the chief himself. The tube had not been there when he went to lunch; it was there when he came back, and so far as could be determined, despite a quite elaborate investigation, no one had been seen to place it there.

In time, still convinced that there had been some sort of hoax played, the postal service delivered the letters to the addresses by special messengers who in their more regular employment were operatives of the World Investigation Bureau.

The addressees were unanimous in their belief the letters were genuine, for in most cases the handwriting was recognized and in every letter there were certain matters in the context which seemed to prove that they were bona fide.

So each of the addressees wrote a letter in reply, and these were inserted in the tube in which the original letters had arrived and the tube was placed meticulously in the exact spot where it had been found on the desk of the postal chief.

Then everyone watched and nothing happened for quite some time, but suddenly the tube was gone and no one had seen it go – it had been there one moment and not there the next.

There remained one question and that one soon was answered. In the matter of a week or two the tube reappeared again, just before the end of office hours. The postal chief had been working away, not paying much attention to what was going on, and suddenly he saw that the tube had come back again.

Once again it held letters and this time the letters were crammed with sheafs of hundred-credit notes, a gift from the marooned spacemen to their relatives, although it should be noted immediately that the spacemen themselves probably did not consider that they were marooned.

The letters acknowledged the receipt of the replies that had been sent from Earth and told more about the planet Kimon and its inhabitants.

And each letter carefully explained how they had hundred-credit notes on Kimon. The notes as they stood, the letters said, were simply counterfeits, made from bills the spacemen had in their pockets, although when Earth's

133

fiscal experts and the Bureau of Investigation men had a look at them there was no way in which you could tell them from the real thing.

But, the letters said, the Kimonian government wished to make right the matter of counterfeiting. To back the currency the Kimonians, within the next short while, would place on deposit with the World Bank materials not only equivalent to their value but enough additional to set up a balance against which more notes could be issued.

There was, the letters explained, no money as such on Kimon, but since Kimon was desirous of employing the men from Earth, there must be some way to pay them, so if it was all right with the World Bank and everyone else concerned . . .

The World Bank did a lot of hemming and hawing and talked about profound fiscal matters and deep economic principles, but all this talk dissolved to nothing when in the matter of a day or two several tons of carefully shielded uranium and a couple of bushels of diamonds were deposited, during the afternoon coffee hour, beside the desk of the bank's president.

With evidence of this sort, there was not much that Earth could do except accept the fact that the planet Kimon was a going concern and that the Earthmen who had landed there were going to stay, and take the entire situation at face value.

The Kimonians, the letters said, were humanoid and had parapsychic powers and had built a culture which was miles ahead of Earth or any other planet so far discovered in the galaxy.

Earth furbished up a ship, hand-picked a corps of its most persuasive diplomats, loaded down the hold with expensive gifts, and sent the whole business out to Kimon.

Within minutes after landing, the diplomats had been quite undiplomatically booted off the planet. Kimon, it appeared, had no desire to ally itself with a second rate, barbaric planet. When it wished to establish diplomatic relationships it would say so. Earth people might come to Kimon if they wished and settle there, but not just any

Earth person. To come to Kimon, the individual would have to possess not only a certain minimum IQ, but must also have an impressive scholastic record.

And that was the way it was left.

You did not go to Kimon simply because you wished to go there – you worked to go to Kimon.

First of all, you had to have the specified IQ rating, and that ruled out 99 per cent or better of Earth's population. Once you had passed the IQ test, you settled down to grueling years of study, and at the end of the years of study you wrote an examination and, once again, most of the aspirants were ruled out. Not more than one in a thousand who took the examination passed.

Year after year Earth men and women dribbled out to Kimon, settled there, prospered, wrote their letters home.

Of those who went out, none came back. Once you had lived on Kimon, you could not bear the thought of going back to Earth.

And yet, in all those years, the sum of knowledge concerning Kimon, its inhabitants and its culture, was very slight indeed. What knowledge there was was compiled from the letters delivered meticulously once each week to the desk of the postal chief in London.

The letters spoke of wages and salaries a hundred times the wages and salaries that were paid on Earth, of magnificent business opportunities, of the Kimonian culture and the Kimonians themselves – but in no detail, of culture or of business or any other factor, were the letters specific.

And perhaps the recipients of the letters did not mind too much the lack of specific information, for almost every letter carried with it a sheaf of notes, all crisp and new, and very, very legal, backed by tons of uranium, bushels of diamonds, stacked bars of gold and other similar knick-knacks deposited from time to time beside the desk of the World Bank's president.

It became, in time, the ambition of every family on the Earth to send at least one relative to Kimon, for a relative on Kimon virtually spelled an assured and sufficient income for the rest of the clan for life.

135

Naturally the legend of Kimon grew. Much that was said about it was untrue, of course. Kimon, the letters protested, did not have streets paved with solid gold, since there were no streets. Nor did Kimonian damsels wear gowns of diamond dust – the damsels of Kimon wore not much of anything.

But to those whose understanding went beyond streets of gold and gowns of diamonds, it was well understood that in Kimon lay possibilities vastly greater than either gold or diamonds. For here was a planet with a culture far in advance of Earth, a people who had schooled themselves or had naturally developed parapsychic powers. On Kimon one could learn the techniques that would revolutionize galactic industry and communications; on Kimon one might discover philosophy that would set mankind overnight on a new and better – and more profitable? – path.

The legend grew, interpreted by each according to his intellect and his way of thought, and grew and grew and grew –

Earth's government was very helpful to those who wished to go to Kimon, for government, as well as individuals, could appreciate the opportunities for the revolution of industry and the evolution of human thought. But since there had been no invitation to grant diplomatic recognition, Earth's government sat and waited, scheming, doing all it could to settle as many of its people on Kimon as was possible. But only the best, for even the densest bureaucrat recognized that on Kimon Earth must put its best foot forward.

Why the Kimonians allowed Earth to send its people was a mystery for which there was no answer. But apparently Earth was the only planet in the galaxy which had been allowed to send its people. The Earthmen and the Kimonians, of course, were both humanoid, but this was not an adequate answer, either, for they were not the only humanoids in the galaxy. For its own comfort Earth assumed that a certain common understanding, a similar outlook, a certain parallel evolutionary trend – with Earth a bit behind of course – between Earth and Kimon might account for Kimon's qualified hospitality.

Be that as it may, Kimon was a galactic El Dorado, a never-never land, a place to get ahead, the place to spend your life, the country at the rainbow's end.

Selden Bishop stood in the parklike area, where the gig had landed him, for Kimon had no spaceports, as it likewise failed to have many other things.

He stood surrounded by his luggage, and watched the gig drive spaceward to rendezvous with the liner's orbit.

When he could see the gig no longer, he sat down on one of his bags and waited.

The park was faintly Earthlike, but the similarity was only in the abstract, for in each particular there was a subtle difference that said this was an alien planet. The trees were too slim and the flowers just a shade too loud and the grass was off a shade or two from the grass you saw on Earth. The birds, if they were birds, were more lizardlike than the birds of Earth and their feathers were put on wrong and weren't quite the color one associated with plumage. The breeze had a faint perfume upon it that was no perfume of Earth, but an alien odor that smelled as a color looked, and Bishop tried to decide, but couldn't, which color it might be.

Sitting on his bag, in the middle of the park, he tried to drum up a little enthusiasm, tried to whistle up some triumph that he finally was on Kimon, but the best that he could achieve was a thankfulness that he'd made it with the twenty still intact.

He would need a little cash to get along on until he could find a job. But, he told himself, he shouldn't have to wait too long before he found a job. The thing, of course, was not to take the first one offered him, but to shop around a little and find the one for which he was best fitted. And that, he knew, might take a little time.

Thinking of it, he wished that he had more than a twenty. He should have allowed himself a bigger margin, but that would have meant something less than the best

137

luggage he could buy and perhaps not enough of it, off-the-rack suits instead of tailored, and all other things accordingly.

It was, he told himself, important that he made the best impression, and sitting there and thinking it over, he couldn't bring himself to regret the money he had spent to make a good impression.

Maybe he should have asked Morley for a loan. Morley would have given him anything he asked and he could have paid it back as soon as he got a job. But he had hated to ask, for to ask, he now admitted, would have detracted from his new-found importance as a man who had been selected to make the trip to Kimon. Everyone, even Morley, looked up to a man who was sent to blast for Kimon, and you couldn't go around asking for a loan or for other favors.

He remembered that last visit he had with Morley, and looking back at it now, he saw that, while Morley was his friend, that last visit had flavored, more or less, of a diplomatic job that Morley had to carry out.

Morley had gone far and was going further in the diplomatic service. He looked like a diplomat and he talked like one and he had a better grasp, old heads at the department said, of Sector nineteen politics and economies that any of the other younger men. He wore a clipped mustache that had a frankly cultivated look, and his hair was always quite in place, and his body, when he walked, was like that of a panther walking.

They had sat in Morley's diggings and had been all comfortable and friendly, and then Morley had got up and paced up and down with his panther walk.

'We've been friends for a long, long time,' said Morley. 'We've been in a lot of scrapes together.'

And the two of them had smiled, remembering some of the scrapes they had been in together.

'When I heard you were going out to Kimon,' Morley said, 'I was pleased about it naturally. I'd be pleased at anything that came your way. But I was pleased, as well,

138

for another reason. I told myself, here, finally, was a man who could do a job and find out what we want.'

'What do you want?' Bishop had asked and, as he remembered it, he had asked if he might be asking whether Morley wanted Scotch or bourbon. Although, come to think of it, he never would have asked that particular question, for all the young men in the alien relations section religiously drank Scotch. But, anyhow, he asked it casually, although he sensed that there was nothing casual at all about the situation.

He could smell the scent of cloak and dagger and he caught a sudden glimpse of huge official worry, and for an instant he was a little cold and scared.

'There must be some way to crack that planet,' Morley had told him, 'but we haven't found it yet. So far as the Kimonians are concerned, none of the rest of us, none of the other planets, officially exist. There's not a single planet accorded diplomatic status. On Kimon there is not a single official representative of any other people. They don't seem to trade with anyone, and yet they must trade with someone, for no planet, no culture can exist in complete self-sufficiency. They must have diplomatic relations somewhere, with someone. There must be some reason, beyond the obvious one that we are an inferior culture, why they do not recognize Earth. For even in the more barbaric days of Earth there was official recognition of many governments and peoples who were cultural inferiors to the recognizing nation.'

'You want me to find out all this?'

'No,' said Morley. 'Not all that. All we want are clues. Somewhere there is the clue that we are looking for, the hint that will tell us what the actual situation is. All we need is the opening wedge – the foot in the door. Give us that and we will do the rest.'

'There have been others,' Bishop told him. 'Thousands of others. I'm not the only one who ever went to Kimon.'

'For the last fifty years or more,' said Morley, 'the section has talked to all the others, before they went out, exactly as I'm talking to you now.'

'And you've got nothing?'

'Nothing,' said Morley. 'Or almost nothing. Or nothing, anyhow, that counted or made any sense.'

'They failed . . .'

'They failed,' Morley told him, 'because once on Kimon they forgot about Earth – well, not forgot about it, that's not entirely it. But they lost all allegiance to it. They were Kimon-blinded.'

'You believe that?'

'I don't know,' said Morley. 'It's the best explanation that we have. The trouble is that we talk to them only once. None of them come back. We can write letters to them, certainly. We can try to jog them – indirectly, of course. But we can't ask them outright.'

'Censorship?'

'Not censorship,' said Morley, 'although they may have that too; but mostly telepathy. The Kimonians would know if we tried to impress anything too forcibly upon their minds. And we can't take the chance of a simple thought undoing all the work that we have done.'

'But you're telling me.'

'You'll forget it,' Morley said. 'You will have several weeks in which you can forget it – push it to the back of your mind. But not entirely – not entirely.'

'I understand,' Bishop told him.

'Don't get me wrong,' said Morley. 'It's nothing sinister. You're not to look for that. It may be just a simple thing. The way we comb our hair. There's some reason – perhaps many little ones. And we must know those reasons.'

Morley had switched it off as quickly as he had begun it, had poured another round of drinks, had sat down again and talked of their school days and of the girls known and of week-ends in the country.

It had been, all in all, a very pleasant evening.

But that had been weeks ago and since then he'd scarcely remembered it and now here he was on Kimon, sitting on one of his bags in the middle of a park, waiting for a welcoming Kimonian to show up.

All the time that he'd been waiting, he had been

prepared for the Kimonian's arrival. He knew what a Kimonian looked like and he should not have been surprised.

But when the native came, he was.

For the native was six feet ten and almost a godlike being, a sculptured humanoid who was, astonishingly, much more human than he had thought to find.

One moment he had sat alone in the little parklike glade and the next the native was standing by his side.

Bishop came to his feet and the Kimonian said, 'We are glad you are here. Welcome to Kimon, sir.'

The native's inflection was as precise and beautiful as his sculptured body.

'Thank you,' Bishop said, and knew immediately that the two words were inadequate and that his voice was slurred and halting compared with the native's voice. And, looking at the Kimonian, he had the feeling that by comparison, he cut a rumpled, seedy figure.

He reached into his pocket for his papers and his fingers were all thumbs, so that he fumbled for them and finally dug them out – dig is the word exactly – and handed them to the waiting being.

The Kimonian flicked them – that was it, flicked them – then he said, 'Mr Selden Bishop. Very glad to know you. Your IQ rating, 160, is very satisfactory. Your examination showing, if I may say so, is extraordinary. Recommendations good. Clearance from Earth in order. And I see you made good time. Very glad to have you.'

'But – ' said Bishop. Then he clamped his mouth tight shut. He couldn't tell this being he'd merely flicked the pages and could not possibly have read them. For, obviously, he had.

'You had a pleasant flight, Mr Bishop?'

'A most pleasant one,' said Bishop and was filled with sudden pride that he could answer so easily and urbanely.

'Your luggage,' said the native, 'is in splendid taste.'

'Why, thank you – ' then was filled with rage. What right had this person to patronize his luggage!

But the native did not appear to notice.

141

'You wish to go to the hotel?'

'If you please,' said Bishop, speaking very tightly, holding himself in check.

'Please allow me,' said the native.

Bishop blurred for just a second – a definite sense of blurring – as if the universe had gone swiftly out of focus, then he was standing, not in the parklike glade, but in a one-man-sized alcove off a hotel lobby, with his bags stacked neatly beside him.

He had missed the triumph before, sitting in the glade, waiting for the native, after the gig had left him, but now it struck him, a heady, drunken triumph that surged through his body and rose in his throat to choke him.

This was Kimon! He was finally on Kimon! After all the years of study, he was here at last – the fabulous place he'd worked for many years to reach.

A high IQ, they'd said behind their half-raised hands – a high IQ and many years of study, and a stiff examination that not more than one in every thousand passed.

He stood in the alcove, with the sense of hiding there, to give himself a moment in which to regain his breath at the splendor of what had finally come to pass, to gain the moment it would take for the unreasoning triumph to have its way with him and go.

For the triumph was something that must not be allowed to last. It was something that he must not show. It was a personal thing and as something personal it must be hidden deep.

He might be one of a thousand back on Earth, but here he stood on no more than equal footing with the ones who had come before him. Perhaps not quite on equal footing, for they would know the ropes and he had yet to learn them.

He watched them in the lobby – the lucky and the fabulous ones who had preceded him, the glittering company he had dreamed about during all the weary years – the company that he would presently join, the ones of Earth who were adjudged fit to go to Kimon.

For only the best must go – the best and smartest and the quickest. Earth must put her best foot forward, for how otherwise would Earth ever persuade Kimon that she was a sister planet?

At first the people in the lobby had been no more than a crowd, a crowd that shone and twinkled, but with that curious lack of personality which goes with a crowd. But now, as he watched, the crowd dissolved into individuals and he saw them, not as a group, but as the men and women he presently would know.

He did not see the bell captain until the native stood in front of him, and the bell captain, if anything, was taller and more handsome than the man who'd met him in the glade.

'Good evening, sir,' the captain said. 'Welcome to the Ritz.'

Bishop started. 'The Ritz? Oh, yes, I had forgotten. This place is the Ritz.'

'We're glad to have you with us,' said the captain. 'We hope your stay will prove to be a long one.'

'Certainly,' said Bishop. 'That is, I hope so, too.'

'We have been notified,' the captain said, 'that you were arriving, Mr Bishop. We took the liberty of reserving rooms for you. I trust they will be satisfactory.'

'I am sure they will be,' Bishop said.

'Perhaps you will want to dress,' the captain said. 'There is still time for dinner.'

'Oh, certainly,' said Bishop. 'Most assuredly I will.' And he wished he had not said it.

'We'll send up the bags,' the captain said. 'No need to register. That is taken care of. If you will permit me, sir.'

The rooms were satisfactory. There were three of them. Sitting in a chair, Bishop wondered how he'd ever pay for them.

Remembering the lonely twenty credits, he was seized with a momentary panic. He'd have to get a job sooner than he planned, for the twenty credits wouldn't go too far with a layout like this one – although he supposed if he asked for credit it would be given him.

But he recoiled from the idea of asking for credit, of being forced to admit that he was short of cash. So far he'd done everything correctly. He'd arrived aboard a liner and not a battered trader; his luggage – what had the native said? – was in splendid taste; his wardrobe was all that could be expected; and he hoped that he'd not communicated to anyone the panic and dismay he'd felt at the luxury of the suite.

He got up from the chair and prowled about the room. There was no carpeting, for the floor itself was soft and yielding, and you left momentary tracks as you walked, but they puffed back and smoothed out almost immediately.

He walked over to a window and stood looking out of it. Evening had fallen and the landscape was covered with a dusty blue – and there was nothing, absolutely nothing, but rolling countryside. There were no roads that he could see and no lights that would have told of other habitations.

Perhaps, he thought, I'm on the wrong side of the building. On the other side there may be streets and roads and homes and shops.

He turned back to the room and looked at it – the Earthlike furniture so quietly elegant that it almost shouted, the beautiful, veined-marble fireplace, the shelves of books, the shine of old wood, the matchless painting hanging on the wall, and the great cabinet that almost filled one end of the room.

He wondered what the cabinet might be. It was a beautiful thing, with an antique look about it and it had a polish – not a wax, but a polish of human hands and time.

He walked toward it.

The cabinet said, 'Drink, sir?'

'I don't mind if I do,' said Bishop, then stopped stock-still, realizing that the cabinet had spoken and he had answered it.

A panel opened in the cabinet and the drink was there.

'Music?' asked the cabinet.

'If you please,' said Bishop.

'Type?'

'Type? Oh, I see. Something gay, but maybe just a little sadness too. Like the blue hour of twilight spreading over Paris. Who was it used that phrase? One of the old writers. Fitzgerald. I'm sure it was Fitzgerald.'

The music told about the blue hour stealing over that city far away on Earth, and there was soft April rain and distant girlish laughter and the shine of the pavement in the slanting rain.

'Is there anything else you wish, sir?' asked the cabinet.

'Nothing at the moment.'

'Very well, sir. You will have an hour to get dressed for dinner.'

He left the room, sipping his drink as he went. The drink had a certain touch to it.

He went into the bedroom and tested the bed, and it was satisfactorily soft. He examined the dresser and the full-length glass and peeked into the bathroom and saw that it was equipped with an automatic shaver and massager, that it had a shower and tub, an exercising machine and a number of other gadgets that he couldn't place.

And the third room. It was almost bare by the standards of the other two. In the center of it stood a chair with great flat arms, and on each of the arms many rows of buttons.

He approached the chair cautiously, wondering what it was – what kind of trap it was – although that was foolish, for there were no traps on Kimon. This was Kimon, the land of opportunity, where a man might make a fortune and live in luxury and rub shoulders with an intelligence and a culture that was the best yet found in the galaxy.

He bent down over the wide arms of the chair and found that each of the buttons was labeled. They were labeled *History*, *Poetry*, *Drama*, *Sculpture*, *Literature*, *Painting*, *Astronomy*, *Philosophy*, *Physics*, *Religions* and many other things. And there were several that were labeled with words he'd never seen and had no meaning to him.

He stood in the room and looked around at its starkness

and saw for the first time that it had no windows, but was just a sort of box – a theater, he decided, or a lecture room. You sat in the chair and pressed a certain button and –

But there was no time for that. An hour to dress for dinner, the cabinet had said, and some of that hour was already gone.

The luggage was in the bedroom and he opened the bag that held his dinner clothes. The jacket was badly wrinkled.

He stood with it in his hands, staring at it. Maybe the wrinkles would hang out. Maybe –

But he knew they wouldn't.

The music stopped and the cabinet asked, 'Is there something that you wish, sir?'

'Can you press a dinner jacket?'

'Surely, sir, I can.'

'How soon?'

'Five minutes,' said the cabinet. 'Give me the trousers, too.'

The bell rang and he went to the door.

A man stood just outside.

'Good evening,' said the man. 'My name is Montague, but they call me Monty.'

'Won't you come in, Monty?'

Monty came in and surveyed the room.

'Nice place,' he said.

Bishop nodded. 'I didn't ask for anything at all. They just gave it to me.'

'Clever, these Kimonians,' said Monty. 'Very clever, yes.'

'My name is Selden Bishop.'

'Just come in?' asked Monty.

'An hour or so ago.'

'All dewed up with what a great place Kimon is?'

'I know nothing about it,' Bishop told him. 'I studied it, of course.'

'I know,' said Monty, looking at him slantwise. 'Just being neighborly. New victim and all that, you know.'

146

Bishop smiled because he didn't quite know what else to do.

'What's your line?' asked Monty.

'Business,' said Bishop. 'Administration's what I'm aiming at.'

'Well, then,' Monty said, 'I guess that lets you out. You wouldn't be interested.'

'In what?'

'In football. Or baseball. Or cricket. Not the athletic type.'

'Never had the time.'

'Too bad,' Monty said. 'You have the build for it.'

The cabinet asked, 'Would the gentleman like a drink?'

'If you please,' said Monty.

'And another one for you, sir?'

'If you please,' said Bishop.

'Go and get dressed,' said Monty. 'I'll sit down and wait.'

'Your jacket and trousers, sir,' said the cabinet.

A door swung open and there they were, cleaned and pressed.

'I didn't know,' said Bishop, 'that you went in for sports out here.'

'Oh, we don't,' said Monty. 'This is a business venture.'

'Business venture?'

'Certainly. Give the Kimonians something to bet on. They might go for it. For a while, at least. You see, they can't bet – '

'I don't see why not – '

'Well, consider for a moment. They have no sports at all, you know. Wouldn't be possible. Telepathy. They'd know three moves ahead what their opponents were about to do. Telekinesis. They could move a piece or a ball or what-have-you without touching a finger to it. They – '

'I think I see,' said Bishop.

'So we plan to get up some teams and put on exhibition matches. Drum up as much enthusiasm as we can. They'll come out in droves to see it. Pay admission. Place bets.

We, of course, will play the bookies and rake off our commissions. It will be a good thing while it lasts.'

'It won't last, of course.'

Monty gave Bishop a long look.

'You catch on fast,' he said. 'You'll get along.'

'Drinks, gentlemen,' the cabinet said.

Bishop got the drinks, gave one of them to his visitor.

'You better let me put you down,' said Monty. 'Might as well rake in what you can. You don't need to know too much about it.'

'All right,' Bishop told him agreeably. 'Go ahead and put me down.'

'You haven't got much money,' Monty said.

'How did you know that?'

'You're scared about this room,' said Monty.

'Telepathy?' asked Bishop.

'You pick it up,' said Monty. 'Just the fringes of it. You'll never be as good as they are. Never. But you pick things up from time to time – a sort of sense that seeps into you. After you've been here long enough.'

'I had hoped that no one would notice.'

'A lot of them will notice, Bishop. Can't help but notice, the way you're broadcasting. But don't let it worry you. We are all friends. Banded against the common enemy, you might say. If you need a loan – '

'Not yet,' said Bishop. 'I'll let you know.'

'Me,' said Monty. 'Me or anyone. We are all friends. We got to be.'

'Thanks.'

'Not at all. Now go ahead and dress. I'll sit and wait for you. I'll bear you down with me. Everyone's waiting to meet you.'

'That's good to know,' said Bishop. 'I felt quite a stranger.'

'Oh, my, no,' said Monty. 'No need to. Not many come, you know. They'll all want to know of Earth.'

He rolled the glass between his fingers.

'How about Earth?' he asked.

'How about – '

148

'Yes, it is still there, of course. How is it getting on? What's the news?'

He had not seen the hotel before. He had caught a confused glimpse of it from the alcove off the lobby, with his luggage stacked up beside him, before the bell captain had showed up and whisked him to his rooms.

But now he saw that it was a strangely substantial fairyland, with fountains and hidden music, with the spidery tracery of rainbows serving as groins and arches, with shimmery columns of glass that caught and reflected and duplicated many times the entire construction of the lobby so that one was at once caught up in the illusion that here was a place that went on and on forever – and at the same time one could cordon off a section of it in one's mind as an intimate corner for a group of friends.

It was illusion and substantiality, beauty and a sense of home – it was, Bishop suspected, all things to all men, and what you wished to make it. A place of utter magic that divorced one from the world and the crudities of the world, with a gaiety that was not brittle and a sentimentality that stopped short of being cheap, and that transmitted a sense of well-being and of self-importance from the very fact of being a part of such a place.

There was no such place on Earth, there could be no such place on Earth, for Bishop suspected that something more than human planning, more than human architectural skill, had gone into its building. You walked in an enchantment and you talked with magic and you felt the sparkle and the shine of the place live within your brain.

'It gets you,' Monty said. 'I always watch the faces of the newcomers when they first walk in it.'

'It wears off after a time,' said Bishop, not believing it.

Monty shook his head. 'My friend, it does not wear off. It doesn't suprise you quite so much, but it stays with you all the time. A human does not live long enough for a place like this to wear thin and commonplace.'

He had eaten dinner in the dining-room, which was old and solemn, with an ancient other worldness and a hushed tiptoe atmosphere, with Kimonian waiters at your elbow, ready to recommend a certain dish or vintage as one that you should try.

Monty had coffee while he ate and there had been others who had come drifting past to stop a moment and welcome him and ask him of Earth, always using a studied casualness, always with a hunger in their eyes that belied the casualness.

'They make me feel at home,' said Monty, 'and they mean it. They are glad when a new one comes.'

He did feel at home — more at home that he had ever felt in his life before, as if already he were beginning to fit in. He had not expected to fit in so quickly and he was slightly astonished at it — for here were all the people he had dreamed of being with, and at last he was with them. You could feel their magnetic force, the personal magnetism that had made them great, great enough to be Kimonworthy, and looking at them he wondered which of them he would get to know, which would be his friends.

He was relieved when he found that he was not expected to pay for his dinner or his drinks, but simply sign a chit, and once he'd caught on to that, everything seemed brighter, for the dinner of itself would have taken quite a hole out of the twenty nestling in his pocket.

With dinner over and with Monty gone somewhere into the crowd, he found himself in the bar, sitting on a stool and nursing a drink that the Kimonian bartender had recommended as being something special.

The girl came out of nowhere and floated up to the stool beside him and she asked, 'What's that you're drinking, friend?'

'I don't know,' said Bishop. He made a thumb toward the man behind the bar. 'Ask him to make you one.'

The bartender heard and got busy with the bottles and the shaker.

'You're fresh from Earth,' said the girl.

'Fresh is the word,' said Bishop.

'It's not so bad,' she said. 'That is, if you don't think about it.'

'I won't think about it,' Bishop promised. 'I won't think of anything.'

'Of course, you do get used to it,' she said. 'After a while you don't mind the faint amusement. You think, what the hell, let them laugh all they want to as long as I have it good. But the day will come – '

'What are you talking about?' asked Bishop. 'Here's your drink. Dip your muzzle into that and – '

'The day will come when we are old to them, when we don't amuse them any longer. When we become *passé*. We can't keep thinking up new tricks. Take my painting, for example – '

'See here,' said Bishop. 'You're talking way above my head.'

'See me in a week from now,' she said. 'The name's Maxine. Just ask to see Maxine. A week from now, we can talk together. So long, buster.'

She floated off the stool and suddenly was gone.

She hadn't touched her drink.

He went up to his rooms and stood for a long time at a window, staring out into the featureless landscape lighted by a moon.

Wonder thundered in his brain, the wonder and the newness and the many questions, the breathlessness of finally being here, of slowly coming to a full realization of the fact that he was here, that he was one of the glittering, fabulous company he had dreamed about for years.

The long grim years peeled off him, the years of books and study, the years of determined driving, the hungry, anxious, grueling years when he had lived a monkish life, mortifying body and soul to drive his intellect.

The years fell off and he felt the newness of himself as well as the newness of the scene. A cleanness and a newness and the sudden glory.

The cabinet finally spoke to him.

'Why don't you try the live-it, sir?'

Bishop swung sharply around. 'You mean . . . ?'

'The third room,' said the cabinet. 'You'll find it most amusing.'

'The live-it!'

'That's right,' said the cabinet. 'You pick it and you live it.'

Which sounded like something out of the Alice books.

'It's safe,' said the cabinet. 'It's perfectly safe. You can come back any time you wish.'

'Thank you,' Bishop said.

He went into the room and sat down in the chair and studied the buttons on the arms. History? Might as well, he told himself. He knew a bit of history. He'd been interested in it and had taken several courses and done a lot of supplemental reading.

He punched the *History* button. A panel in the wall before the chair lit up and a face appeared – the face of a Kimonian, the bronzed and golden face, the classic beauty of the race.

Aren't any of them plain? Bishop wondered. None of them ugly or crippled, like the rest of humanity?

'What type of history, sir?' the face in the screen asked him.

'Type?'

'Galactic, Kimonian, Earth – almost any place you wish.'

'Earth, please,' said Bishop.

'Specifications?'

'England,' said Bishop, '14th October, 1066. A place called Senlac.'

And he was there.

He was no longer in the room with its single chair and its four bare walls, but he stood upon a hill in sunny autumn weather with the gold and red of trees and the blueness of the haze and the shouts of men.

He stood rooted in the grass that blew upon the hillside and saw that the grass had turned to hay with its age and sunshine – and out beyond the grass and hill, grouped down on the plain, was a ragged line of horsemen, with the sun upon their helmets and flashing on their shields, with the leopard banners curling in the wind.

It was October 14 and it was Saturday and on the hill stood Harold's hosts behind their locked shield wall, and before the sun had set new forces would have been put in motion to shape the course of empire.

Taillefer, he thought, Taillefer will ride in the fore of William's charge, singing the *Chanson de Roland* and wheeling his sword into the air so that it becomes a wheel of fire to lead the others on.

The Normans charged and there was no Taillefer. No one wheeled his sword into the air, there was no singing. There was merely shouting and the hoarse crying of men riding to their death.

The horsemen were charging directly at him, and he wheeled and tried to run, but he could not outrun them and they were upon him. He saw the flash of polished hoofs and the cruel steel of the shoes upon the hoofs, the glinting lance point, the swaying, jouncing scabbard, the red and green and yellow of the cloaks, the dullness of the armor, the open roaring mouths of men – and they were upon him. And passing through him and over him as if he were not there.

He stopped stock-still, heart hammering in his chest, and, as if from somewhere far off, he felt the wind of the charging horses that were running all around him.

Up the hill there were hoarse cries of 'Ut! Ut!' and the high, sharp ring of steel. Dust was rising all around him and somewhere off to the left a dying horse was screaming. Out of the dust a man came running down the hill. He staggered and fell and got up and ran again and Bishop could see that blood poured out of the ripped armor and washed down across the metal, spraying the dead, sere grass as he ran down the hill.

The horses came back again, some of them riderless, running with their necks outstretched, with the reins flying in the wind, with foam dashing from their mouths.

One man sagged in the saddle and fell off, but his foot caught in the stirrup and his horse, shying, dragged him sidewise.

Up on top of the hill the Saxon square was cheering and

through the settling dust he saw the heap of bodies that lay outside the shield wall.

Let me out of here! Bishop was screaming to himself. *How do I get out of here! Let me out —*

He was out, back in the room again, with its single chair and the four blank walls.

He sat there quietly and he thought: *There was no Taillefer. No one who rode and sang and tossed the sword in the air. The tale of Taillefer was no more than the imagination of some copyist who had improved upon the tale to while away his time.*

But men had died. They had run down the hill, staggering with their wounds, and died. They had fallen from their horses and been dragged to death by their frightened mounts. They had come crawling down the hill, with minutes left of life and with a whimper in their throats.

He stood up and his hands were shaking. He walked unsteadily into the next room.

'You are going to bed, sir?' asked the cabinet.

'I think I will,' said Bishop.

'Very good, then, sir. I'll lock up and put out.'

'That's very good of you.'

'Routine, sir,' said the cabinet. 'Is there anything you wish?'

'Not a thing,' said Bishop. 'Good night.'

'Good night,' said the cabinet.

In the morning he went to the employment agency which he found in one corner of the hotel lobby.

There was no one around but a Kimonian girl, a tall, statuesque blonde, but with a grace to put to shame the most petite of humans. A woman, Bishop thought, jerked out of some classic Grecian myth, a blonde goddess come to life and beauty. She didn't wear the flowing Grecian robe, but she could have. She wore, truth to tell, but little, and was all the better for it.

'You are new,' she said.

He nodded.

'Wait, I know,' she said. She looked at him. 'Selden Bishop, age twenty-nine Earth years, IQ, 160.'

'Yes, ma'am,' he said.

She made him feel as if he should bow and scrape.

'Business administration, I understand,' she said.

He nodded bleakly.

'Please sit down, Mr Bishop, and we will talk this over.'

He sat down and he was thinking: It isn't right for a beautiful girl to be so big and husky. Or so competent.

'You'd like to get started doing something,' said the girl.

'That's the thought I had.'

'You specialized in business administration. I'm afraid there aren't many openings in that particular field.'

'I wouldn't expect too much to start with,' Bishop told her with what he felt was a becoming modesty and a realistic outlook. 'Almost anything at all, until I can prove my value.'

'You'd have to start at the very bottom. And it would take years of training. Not in method only, but in attitude and philosophy.'

'I wouldn't mind . . .' He hesitated. He had meant to say that he wouldn't mind. But he would mind. He would mind a lot.

'But I spent years,' he said. 'I know – '

'Kimonian business?'

'Is it so much different?'

'You know all about contracts, I suppose.'

'Certainly I do.'

'There is no such thing as a contract on all of Kimon.'

'But – '

'There is no need of any.'

'Integrity?'

'That, and other things as well.'

'Other things?'

'You wouldn't understand.'

'Try me.'

'It would be useless, Mr Bishop. New concepts entirely so far as you're concerned. Of behavior. Of motives. On Earth, profit is the motive – '

'Isn't it here?'

'In part. A very small part.'

155

'The other motives – '

'Cultural development for one. Can you imagine an urge to cultural development as powerful as the profit motive?'

Bishop was honest about it. 'No, I can't,' he said.

'Here,' she said, 'it is the more powerful of the two. But that's not all. Money is another thing. We have no actual money. No coin that changes hands.'

'But there is money. Credit notes.'

'For the convenience of your race alone,' she said. 'We created your money values and your evidence of wealth so that we could hire your services and pay you – and I might add that we pay you well. We have gone through all the motions. The currency that we create is as valid as anywhere else in the galaxy. It's backed by deposits in Earth's banks and it is legal tender so far as you're concerned. But Kimonians themselves do not employ money.'

Bishop floundered. 'I can't understand,' he said.

'Of course you can't,' she said. 'It's an entirely new departure for you. Your culture is so constituted that there must be a certain physical assurance of each person's wealth and worth. Here we do not need that physical assurance. Here each person carries in his head the simple bookkeeping of his worth and debts. It is there for him to know. It is there for his friends and business associates to see at any time they wish.'

'It isn't business, then,' said Bishop. 'Not business as I think of it.'

'Exactly,' said the girl.

'But I am trained for business, I spent – '

'Years and years of study. But on Earth's methods of business, not on Kimon's.'

'But there are businessmen here. Hundreds of them.'

'Are there?' she asked. She was smiling at him. Not a superior smile, nor a taunting one – just smiling at him.

'What you need,' she said, 'is contact with Kimonians. A chance to get to know your way around. An opportunity

156

to appreciate our point of view and get the hang of how we do things.'

'That sounds all right,' said Bishop. 'How do I go about it?'

'There have been instances,' said the girl, 'when Earth people sold their services as companions.'

'I don't think I'd care much for that. It sounds — well, like baby sitting or reading to old ladies or . . .'

'Can you play an instrument or sing?'

Bishop shook his head.

'Paint? Draw? Dance?'

He couldn't do any of them.

'Box, perhaps,' she said. 'Physical combat. That is popular at times, if it's not overdone.'

'You mean prize fighting?'

'I think that is one way you describe it.'

'No, I can't,' said Bishop.

'That doesn't leave much,' she said, as she picked up some papers.

'Transportation?' he asked.

'Transportation is a personal matter.'

And of course, it was, he told himself. With telekinesis you could transport yourself or anything you might have a mind to move — without mechanical aid.

'Communication,' he said weakly. 'I suppose that is the same?'

She nodded.

With telepathy, it would be.

'You know about transportation and communications, Mr Bishop?'

'Earth variety,' said Bishop. 'No good here, I gather.'

'None at all,' she said. 'Although we might arrange a lecture tour. Some of us would help you put your material together.'

Bishop shook his head. 'I can't talk,' he said.

She got up.

'I'll check around,' she said. 'Drop in again. We'll find something that you'll fit.'

'Thanks,' he said and went back to the lobby.

*

He went for a walk.

There were no roads or paths. There was nothing. The hotel stood on the plain and there was nothing else. No buildings around it. No village. No roads. Nothing.

It stood there, huge and ornate and lonely, like a misplaced thing. It stood stark against the skyline, for there were no other buildings to blend into it and soften it and it looked like something that someone in a hurry had dumped down and left.

He struck out across the plain toward some trees that he thought must mark a watercourse and he wondered why there were no paths or roads – but suddenly he knew why there were no paths or roads.

He thought about the years he had spent cramming business administration into his brain and he remembered the huge book of excerpts from the letters written home from Kimon hinting at big business deals, at responsible positions.

And the thought struck him that there was one thing in common in all of the excerpts in the book – that the deals and positions were always hinted at, that no one had ever told exactly what he did.

Why did they do it? he asked himself. Why did they fool us all?

Although, of course, there might be more to it than he knew. He had been on Kimon for somewhat less than a full day's time. I'll look around, the Grecian blonde had said – I'll look around, we'll find something that you'll fit.

He went on across the plain and reached the line of trees and found the stream. It was a prairie stream, a broad, sluggish flow of crystal water between two grassy banks. Lying on his stomach to peer into the depths, he saw the flash of fishes far below him.

He took off his shoes and dangled his feet in the water and kicked a little to make the water splash, and he thought: They know all about us. They know about our life and culture. They know about the leopard banners and how Senlac must have looked on Saturday, 14th

October, 1066, with the hosts of England massed upon the hilltop and the hosts of William on the plain below.

They know what makes us tick and they let us come, and because they let us come there must be some value in us.

What had the girl said, the girl who had floated to the stool and then left with her drink still standing and untouched? Faint amusement, she had said. You get used to it, she had said. If you don't think too much about it, you get used to it.

See me in a week, she had said. In a week you and I can talk. And she had called him buster.

Well, maybe she had a right to call him that. He had been starry-eyed and a sort of eager beaver. And probably ignorant-smug.

They know about us and how do they know about us?

Senlac might have been staged, but he didn't think so — there was a strange, grim reality about it that got under your skin, a crawling sort of feeling that told you it was true, that that was how it happened and had been. That there had been no Taillefer and that a man had died with his guts dragging in the grass and that the Englishmen had cried 'Ut! Ut!' which might have meant almost anything at all, or nothing, but probably had meant 'Out.'

He sat there, cold and lonely, wondering how they did it. How they had made it possible for a man to punch a button and to live a scene long dead, to see the deaths of men who had long been dust mingled with the earth.

There was no way to know, of course. There was no use to guess.

Technical information, Morley Reed had said, that would revolutionize our entire economic pattern.

He remembered Morley pacing up and down the room and saying, 'We must find out about them. We must find out.'

And there was a way to find out. There was a splendid way.

He took his feet out of the water and dried them with

handfuls of grass. He put his shoes back on and walked back to the hotel that sat by itself.

The blonde goddess was still at her desk in the employment bureau.

'About the baby-sitting job,' he said.

She looked startled for a moment – terribly, almost childishly startled – but her face slid swiftly back to its goddess mask.

'Yes, Mr Bishop.'

'I've thought it over,' he said. 'If you have that kind of job I'll take it.'

He lay in bed, sleepless, for a long time that night and took stock of himself and of the situation and he came to a decision that it might not be so bad as he thought it was.

There were jobs to be had, apparently. The Kimonians even seemed anxious that you should get a job. And even if it weren't the kind of work a man might want, or the kind that he was fitted for, at least it would be a start. From that first foothold a man could go up – a clever man, that is. And all the men and women, all the Earthians on Kimon, certainly were clever. If they weren't clever, they wouldn't be there to start with.

All of them seemed to be getting along. He had not seen either Monty or Maxine that evening but he had talked to others, and all of them seemed to be satisfied – or at least they kept up the appearance of being satisfied. If there were general dissatisfaction, Bishop told himself, there wouldn't even be the appearance of being satisfied, for there is nothing that an Earthian likes better than some quiet and mutual griping. And he had heard none of it – none of it at all.

He had heard some more talk about the starting of the athletic teams and had talked to several men who had been enthusiastic about it as a source of revenue.

He had talked to another man named Thomas who was a gardening expert at one of the big Kimonian estates, and the man had talked for an hour or more on the growing of exotic flowers. There had been a little man named

160

Williams who had sat in the bar beside him and had told him enthusiastically of his commission to write a book of ballads based on Kimonian history and another man named Jackson who was executing a piece of statuary for one of the native families.

If a man could get a satisfactory job, Bishop thought, life could be pleasant here on Kimon.

Take the rooms he had. Beautiful appointments, much better than he could expect at home. A willing cabinet robot who dished up drinks and sandwiches, who pressed clothes, turned out and locked up, and anticipated your no more than half-formed wish. And the room – the room with the four blank walls and the single chair with the buttons on its arms. There, in that room, was instruction and entertainment and adventure. He had made a bad choice in picking the Battle of Hastings for the first test of it, he knew now. But there were other places, other times, other more pleasant and less bloody incidents that one could experience.

It was an experience, too – and not merely seeing. He had really been walking on the hilltop. He had tried to dodge the charging horses, although there'd been no reason to, for apparently, even in the midst of a happening, you stood by some special dispensation as a thing apart, as an interested but unreachable observer.

And there were, he told himself, many happenings that would be worth observing. One could live out the entire history of mankind, from the prehistoric dawnings to the day before yesterday – and not only the history of mankind, but the history of other things as well, for there had been other categories of experience offered – Kimonian and galactic – in addition to Earth.

Some day, he thought, I will walk with Shakespeare. Some day I'll sail with Columbus. Or travel with Prester John and find the truth about him.

For it was truth. You could sense the truth.

And how the truth? That he could not know. But it all boiled down to the fact that while conditions might be strange, one still could make a life of it.

161

And conditions would be strange, for this was an alien land and one that was immeasurably in advance of Earth in culture and in its technology. Here there was no need of artificial communications or of mechanical transportation. Here there was no need of contracts since the mere fact of telepathy would reveal one man to another, so there'd be no need of contracts.

You'll have to adapt, Bishop told himself. You'd have to adapt to play the Kimon game, for they were the ones who would set the rules. Unbidden he had entered their planet, and they had let him stay, and, staying, it followed that he must conform.

'You are restless, sir,' said the cabinet from the other room.

'Not restless,' Bishop said. 'Just thinking.'

'I can supply you with a sedative. A very mild and pleasant sedative.'

'Not a sedative,' said Bishop.

'Then, perhaps,' the cabinet said, 'you would permit me to sing you a lullaby.'

'By all means,' said Bishop. 'A lullaby is just the thing I need.'

So the cabinet sang him a lullaby and after a time Bishop went to sleep.

The Kimonian goddess at the employment bureau told him next morning that there was a job for him.

'A new family,' she said.

Bishop wondered if he should be glad that it was a new family or if it would have been better if it had been an old one.

'They've never had a human before,' she said.

'It's fine of them,' said Bishop, 'to finally take one in.'

'The salary,' said the goddess, 'is one hundred credits a day.'

'One hundred – '

'You will only work during days,' she said. 'I'll teleport you there each morning and in the evening they'll teleport you back.'

Bishop gulped. 'One hundred – What am I to do?'

'A companion,' said the goddess. 'But you needn't worry. We'll keep an eye on them and if they mistreat you . . .'

'Mistreat me?'

'Work you too hard – '

'Miss,' said Bishop, 'for a hundred bucks a day I'd – '

She cut him short. 'You will take the job?'

'Most gladly,' Bishop said.

'Permit me – ' The universe came unstuck, then slapped back together.

He was standing in an alcove and in front of him was a woodland glen with a waterfall, and from where he stood he could smell the cool, mossy freshness of the tumbling water. There were ferns and trees, huge trees like the gnarled oaks the illustrators like to draw to illustrate King Arthur and Robin Hood and other tales of very early Britain – the kind of oaks from which the Druids had cut the mistletoe.

A path ran along the stream and up the incline down which the waterfall came tumbling, and there was a blowing wind that carried music and perfume.

A girl came down the path and she was Kimonian, but she didn't seem as tall as the others he had seen and there was something a little less goddess-like about her.

He caught his breath and watched her, and for a moment he forgot that she was Kimonian and thought of her only as a pretty girl who walked a woodland path. She was beautiful, he told himself – she was lovely.

She saw him and clapped her hands.

'You must be he,' she said.

He stepped out of the cubicle.

'We have been waiting for you,' she told him. 'We hoped there'd be no delay, that they'd send you right along.'

'My name,' said Bishop, 'is Selden Bishop and I was told – '

'Of course you are the one,' she said. 'You needn't even tell me. It's lying in your mind.'

163

She waved an arm about her.

'How do you like your house?' she asked.

'House?'

'Of course, silly. This. Naturally, it's only the living-room. Our bedrooms are up in the mountains. But we changed this just yesterday. Everyone worked so hard at it. I do hope you like it. Because you see, it is from your planet. We thought it might make you feel at home.'

'House,' he said again.

She reached out a hand and laid it on his arm.

'You're all upset,' she said. 'You don't begin to understand.'

Bishop shook his head. 'I just arrived the other day.'

'But you do like it?'

'Of course I do,' said Bishop. 'It's something out of the old Arthurian legend. You'd expect to see Lancelot or Guinevere or some of the others riding through the woods.'

'You know the stories?'

'Of course I know the stories. I read my Tennyson.'

'And you will tell them to us.'

He looked at her, a little startled. 'You mean you want to hear them?'

'Why, yes, of course we do. What did we get you for?'

And that was it, of course. What had they got him for?

'You want me to begin right now?'

'Not now,' she said. 'There are the others you must meet. My name is Elaine. That's not exactly it, of course. It is something else, but Elaine is as close as you'll ever come to saying it.'

'I could try the other name. I'm proficient at the languages.'

'Elaine is good enough,' she said carelessly. 'Come along.'

He fell in behind her on the path and followed up the incline.

And as he walked along, he saw that it was indeed a house – that the trees were pillars holding up an artificial sky that somehow failed to look very artificial and that the

164

aisles between the trees ended in great windows which looked out on the barren plain.

But the grass and flowers, the moss and ferns, were real and he had a feeling that the trees must be real as well.

'It doesn't matter if they're real or not,' said Elaine. 'You couldn't tell the difference.'

They came to the top of the incline into a parklike place, where the grass was cut so closely and looked so velvety that he wondered for a moment if it were really grass.

'It is,' Elaine told him.

'You catch everything I think,' he said. 'Isn't – ?'

'Everything,' said Elaine.

'Then I mustn't think.'

'Oh, but we want you to,' she told him. 'That is part of it.'

'Part of what you got me for?'

'Exactly,' said the girl.

In the middle of the parklike area was a sort of pagoda, a flimsy thing that seemed to be made out of light and shadow rather than of substance, and around it were half a dozen people.

They were laughing and chatting and the sound was like the sound of music – very happy, but at the same time sophisticated music.

'There they are,' cried Elaine. 'Come along.'

She ran and her running was like flying and his breath caught in his throat at the slimness and the grace of her.

He ran after her and there was no grace in his running. He could feel the heaviness. It was a gallop rather than a run, an awkward lope in comparison to the running of Elaine.

Like a dog, he thought. Like an overgrown puppy trying to keep up, falling over his own feet, with its tongue hanging out and panting.

He tried to run more gracefully and he tried to erase the thinking from his mind.

Mustn't think. Mustn't think at all. They catch everything. They will laugh at you.

They *were* laughing at him. He could feel their laughter,

the silent, gracious amusement that was racing in their minds.

She reached the group and waited. 'Hurry up,' she called and while her words were kindly, he could feel the amusement in the words.

He hurried. He pounded down upon them. He arrived somewhat out of breath. He felt winded and sweaty and extremely uncouth.

'This is the one they sent us,' said Elaine. 'His name is Bishop. Is that not a lovely name?'

They watched him, nodding gravely.

'He will tell us stories,' said Elaine. 'He knows the stories that go with a place like this.'

They were looking kindly at him, but he could sense the covert amusement, growing by the moment.

She said to Bishop. 'This is Paul. And that one over there is Jim. Betty. Jane. George. And the one on the end is Mary.'

'You understand,' said Jim, 'those are not our names.'

'They are approximations,' said Elaine. 'The best that I could do.'

'They are as close,' said Jane, 'as he can pronounce them.'

'If you'd only give me a chance,' said Bishop, then stopped short.

That was what they wanted. They wanted him to protest and squirm. They wanted him to be uncomfortable.

'But of course we don't,' said Elaine.

Mustn't think. Must try to keep from thinking. They catch everything.

'Let's all sit down,' said Betty. 'Bishop will tell us stories.'

'Perhaps,' Jim said to him, 'you will describe your life on Earth. I should be quite interested.'

'I understand you have a game called chess,' said George. 'We can't play games, of course. You know why we can't. But I'd be very interested in discussing with you the technique and philosophy of chess.'

'One at a time,' said Elaine. 'First he will tell us stories.'

166

They sat down on the grass, in a ragged circle. All of them were looking at him, waiting for him to start.

'I don't quite know where to start,' he said.

'Why, that's obvious,' said Betty. 'You start at the beginning.'

'Quite right,' said Bishop.

He took a deep breath.

'Once, long ago, in the island of Britain, there was a great king, whose name was Arthur — '

'Yclept,' said Jim.

'You've read the stories?'

'The word was in your mind.'

'It's an old word, an archaic word. In some versions of the tales — '

'I should be most interested sometimes to discuss the word with you,' said Jim.

'Go on with your story,' said Elaine.

He took another deep breath.

'Once, long ago, in the island of Britain, there was a great king whose name was Arthur. His queen was Guinevere and Lancelot was his staunchest knight . . .'

He found the writer in the desk in the living room and pulled it out. He sat down to write a letter.

He typed the salutation. *Dear Morley*

He got up and began pacing up and down the room.

What would he tell him? What could he tell him? That he had safely arrived and he had a job? That the job paid a hundred credits a day — ten times more than a man in his position could earn at any Earth job?

He went back to the writer again. He wrote:

Just a note to let you know that I arrived safely and already have a job. Not too good a job perhaps, but it pays a hundred a day and that's better than I could have done on Earth.

He got up and walked again. There had to be more than that. More than just a paragraph. He sweated as he walked. What could he tell him?

He went back to the writer again:

In order to learn the conditions and the customs more quickly

I have taken a job which will keep me in touch with the Kimonians. I find them to be a fine people, but sometimes a little hard to understand. I have no doubt that before too long I shall get to understand them and have a genuine liking for them.

He pushed back his chair and stared at what he'd written.

It was, he told himself, like any one of a thousand other letters he had read.

He pictured in his mind those other thousand people, sitting down to write their first letter from Kimon, searching in their mind for the polite little fables, for the slightly colored lie, for the balm that would salve their pride. Hunting for the words that would not reveal the entire truth:

I have a job of entertaining and amusing a certain family. I tell them stories and let them laugh at me. I do this because I will not admit that the fable of Kimon is a booby trap and that I've fallen into it –

No, it would never do to write that. Nor to write:

I'm sticking on in spite of them. So long as I make a hundred a day, they can laugh as much as they want to laugh. I'm staying here and cleaning up no matter what . . .

Back home he was one of a thousand. Back home they talked of him in whispers because he made the grade.

And the businessmen on board the ship, saying to him, 'The one who cracks this Kimon business is the one who'll have it big,' and talking in terms of billions if he ever needed backing.

He remembered Morley pacing up and down the room. A foot in the door, he'd said. Some way to crack them. Some way to understand them. Some little thing – no big thing, but some little thing. Anything at all except the deadpan face that Kimon turns toward us.

Somehow he had to finish the letter. He couldn't leave it hanging and he had to write it.

He turned back to the writer.

I'll write you later at greater length. At the moment I'm rushed.

He frowned at it. But whatever he wrote, it would be
168

wrong. This was no worse than any of another dozen things that he might write.

Must rush off to a conference . . . Have an appointment with a client . . . Some papers to go through . . . All of them were wrong.

What was a man to do? He wrote: *Think of you often. Write me when you can.*

Morley would write him. An enthusiastic letter, a letter with a fine shade of envy tingeing it, the letter of a man who wanted to be, but couldn't be, on Kimon.

For everyone wanted to go to Kimon. That was the hell of it.

You couldn't tell the truth, when everyone would give his good right arm to go.

You couldn't tell the truth when you were a hero and the truth would turn you into a galactic heel.

And the letters from home, the prideful letters, the envious letters, the letters happy with the thought you were doing so well — all of these would be only further chains to bind you to Kimon and to the Kimon lie.

He said to the cabinet, 'How about a drink?'

'Yes, sir,' said the cabinet. 'Coming right up, sir.'

'A long one,' said Bishop. 'And a strong one.'

'Long and strong it is, sir.'

He met her in the bar.

'Why, if it isn't buster!' she said, as though they met there often.

He sat on the stool beside her. 'That week is almost up,' he said.

She nodded. 'We've been watching you. You're standing up real well.'

'You tried to tell me.'

'Forget it,' said the girl. 'Just a mistake of mine. It's a waste of time telling any of them. But you looked intelligent and not quite dry behind the ears. I took pity on you.'

She looked at him over the rim of her glass. 'I shouldn't have,' she said.

'I should have listened.'

'They never do,' said Maxine.

'There's another thing,' he said. 'Why hasn't it leaked out? Oh sure, I have written letters, too. I didn't admit what it was like. Neither did you. Nor the man next to you. But someone, in all these years we've been here – '

'We are all alike,' she said. 'Alike as peas in the pod. We are the appointed, the hand-picked – stubborn, vanity-stricken, scared. All of us got here. In spite of hell and high water we got here. We let nothing stand in our way and we made it. We beat the others out. They're waiting back there on Earth – the ones that we beat out. They'll never be quite the same again. Don't you understand it? They had pride, too, and it was hurt. There's nothing they would like better than to know what it's really like. That's what all of us think of when we sit down to write a letter. We think of the belly laughs of those other thousands. The quiet smirks. We think of ourselves skulking, making ourselves small so no one will notice us – ' She balled a fist and rapped against his shirt front.

'That's the answer, buster. That's why we never write the truth. That's why we don't go back.'

'But it's been going on for years. For almost a hundred years. In all that time someone should have cracked – '

'And lost all this?' she asked. 'Lost the easy living. The good drinking. The fellowship of lost souls. And the hope. Don't forget that. Always the hope that Kimon can be cracked.'

'Can it?'

'I don't know. But if I were you, buster, I wouldn't count on it.'

'But it's no kind of life for decent – '

'Don't say it. We aren't decent people. We are scared and weak, every one of us. And with good reason.'

'But the life . . .'

'You don't lead a decent life, if that was what you were about to say. There's no stability in us. Children? A few of us have children, and it's not so bad for the children as it is for us, because they know nothing else. A child who is

170

born a slave is better off, mentally, than a man who once knew freedom.'

'We aren't slaves,' said Bishop.

'Of course not,' Maxine said. 'We can leave any time we want to. All we have to do is walk up to a native and say, "I want to go back to Earth." That's all you need to do. Any single one of them could send you back – *swish* – just as they send the letters, just as they whisk you to your work or to your room.'

'But no one has gone back.'

'Of course no one has,' she said.

They sat there, sipping at their drinks.

'Remember what I told you,' she said. 'Don't think. That's the way to beat it. Never think about it. You have it good. You never had it so good. Soft living. Easy living. Nothing to worry about. The best kind of life there is.'

'Sure,' said Bishop. 'Sure, that's the way to do it.'

She slanted her eyes at him. 'You're catching on,' she said. They had another round.

Over in the corner a group had got together and was doing some impromptu singing. A couple were quarreling a stool or two away.

'It's too noisy in this place,' Maxine said. 'Want to see my paintings?'

'Your paintings?'

'The way I make a living. They are pretty bad, but no one knows the difference.'

'I'd like to see them.'

'Grab hold then.'

'Grab . . .'

'My mind, you know. Nothing physical about it. No use riding elevators.'

He gaped at her.

'You pick it up,' said Maxine. 'You never get too good. But you pick up a trick or two.'

'But how do I go about it?'

'Just let loose,' she said. 'Dangle. Mentally, that is. Try to reach out to me. Don't try to help. You can't.'

He dangled and reached out, wondering if he was doing it the way it should be done.

The universe collapsed and then came back together.

They were standing in another room.

'That was a silly thing for me to do,' Maxine said. 'Some day I'll slip a cog and get stuck in a wall or something.'

Bishop drew a deep breath. 'Monty could read me just a little,' he said. 'Said you picked it up – just at the fringes.'

'You never get too good,' said Maxine. 'Humans aren't . . . well, aren't ripe for it, I guess. It takes millennium to develop it.'

He looked around him and whistled.

'Quite a place,' he said.

It was all of that. It didn't seem to be a room at all, although it had furniture. The walls were hazed in distance and to the west were mountains peaked with snow, and to the east a very sylvan river and there were flowers and flowering bushes everywhere, growing from the floor. A deep blue dusk filled the room and somewhere off in the distance there was an orchestra.

A cabinet-voice said, 'Anything, madam?'

'Drinks,' said Maxine. 'Not too strong. We've been hitting the bottle.'

'Not too strong,' said the cabinet. 'Just a moment, madam.'

'Illusion,' Maxine said. 'Every bit of it. But a nice illusion. Want a beach? It's waiting for you if you just think of it. Or a polar cap. Or a desert. Or an old chateau. It's waiting in the wings.'

'Your painting must pay off,' he said.

'Not my painting. My irritation. Better start getting irritated, buster. Get down in the dumps. Start thinking about suicide. That's a sure-fire way to do it. Presto, you're kicked upstairs to a better suite of rooms. Anything to keep you happy.'

'You mean the Kimonians automatically shift you?'

'Sure. You're a sucker to stay down there where you are.'

'I like my layout,' he told her. 'But this . . .'

172

She laughed at him. 'You'll catch on,' she said.

The drinks arrived.

'Sit down,' Maxine said. 'Want a moon?'

There was a moon.

'Could have two or three,' she said. 'but that would be overdoing it. One moon seems more like Earth. Seems more comfortable.'

'There must be a limit somewhere,' Bishop said. 'They can't keep on kicking you upstairs indefinitely. There must come a time when even the Kimonians can't come up with anything that is new and novel.'

'You wouldn't live long enough,' she told him, 'for that to come about. That's the way with all you new ones. You underestimate the Kimonians. You think of them as people, as Earth people who know just a little more. They aren't that, at all. They're alien. They're as alien as a spider-man despite their human form. They conform to keep contact with us.'

'But why do they want to keep contact with us? Why – '

'Buster,' she said. 'That's the question that we never ask. That's the one that can drive you crazy.'

He had told them about the human custom of going out on picnics and the idea was one that they had never thought of, so they adopted it with childish delight.

They had picked a wild place, a tumbled mountain area filled with deep ravines, clothed in flowers and trees. There was a mountain brook with water that was as clear as glass and as cold as ice.

They had played games and romped. They had swum and sunbathed and they had listened to his stories, sitting in a circle, needling him and interrupting him, picking arguments.

But he had laughed at them, not openly, but deep inside himself, for he knew now that they meant no harm but merely sought amusement.

Weeks before, he had been insulted and outraged and humiliated, but as the days went on he had adapted to it –

had forced himself to adapt. If they wished a clown, then he would be a clown. If he were court fool, with bells and parti-colored garments, then he must wear the colors well and keep the bells ringing merrily.

There was occasional maliciousness in them, and some cruelty, but no lasting harm. And you could get along with them, he told himself, if you just knew how to do it.

When evening came they had built a fire and had sat around it and had talked and laughed and joked, for once leaving him alone. Elaine and Betty had been nervous. Jim had laughed at them for their nervousness.

'No animal will come near a fire,' he said.

'There are animals?' Bishop had asked.

'A few,' said Jim. 'Not many of them left.'

He had lain there, staring at the fire, listening to their voices, glad that for once they were leaving him alone. Like a dog must feel, he thought. Like a pup hiding in a corner from a gang of rowdy children who were always mauling it.

He watched the fire and remembered other days — outings in the country and walking trips when they had built a fire and lain around it, staring at the sky, seeing the old familiar skies of Earth.

And here again was another fire. And here, again, a picnic. The fire was Earth and so was the picnic — for the people of Kimon did not know of picnics. They did not know of picnics and there might be many other things of which they likewise did not know. Many other things, perhaps. Barbaric, folkish things.

Don't look for the big things, Morley had said that night. Watch for the little things, for the little clues.

They liked Maxine's paintings because they were primitives. Primitives, perhaps, but not very good ones. Could it be that paintings were also something the Kimonians had not known until the Earthmen came?

Were there, after all, chinks in the Kimonian armor? Little chinks like picnics and paintings and many other little things for which they valued the visitors from Earth?

174

Somewhere in those chinks might be the answer that he sought for Morley.

He lay and thought, forgetting to shield his mind, forgetting that he should not think because his thoughts lay open to them.

Their voices had faded away and there was a solemn nighttime quiet. Soon, he thought, we'll all be going back – they to their homes and I to the hotel. How far away? he wondered. Half a world or less? And yet they'd be there in the instant of a thought.

Someone, he thought, should put more wood on the fire. He roused himself to do it, standing up. And it was not until then that he saw he was alone.

He stood there, trying to quiet his terror. They had gone away and left him. They had forgotten him. But that couldn't be. They'd simply slipped off in the dark. Up to some prank, perhaps. Trying to scare him. Talking about the animals and then slipping out of sight while he lay dreaming at the fire. Waiting now, just outside the circle of the firelight, watching him, drinking in his thoughts, reveling in his terror.

He found wood and put it on the fire. It caught and blazed. He sat down nonchalantly, but he found that his shoulders were hunched instinctively, that the terror of aloneness in an alien world still sat beside him by the fire.

Now, for the first time, he realized the alienness of Kimon. It had not seemed alien before except for those few minutes he had waited in the park after the gig had landed him, and even then it had not been as alien as an alien planet should be, because he knew that he was being met, that there would be someone along to take care of him.

That was it, he thought. Someone to take care of me. We're taken care of – well and lavishly. We're sheltered and guarded and pampered – that was it, *pampered*. And for what reason?

Any minute now they'd tire of their game and come back into the circle of the firelight. Maybe, he told himself, I should give them their money's worth. Maybe I should act scared, maybe I should shout out for them to come and get me, maybe I should glance around out into the darkness, as if I were afraid of those animals that they talked about. They hadn't talked too much, of course. They were too clever for that, far too clever. Just a passing remark about existent animals, then on to something else. No stressing it, not laying it on too thick. Not overdoing it. Just planting a suggestion that there were animals one could be afraid of.

He sat and waited, not so scared as he had been before, having rationalized away the fear that he first had felt. Like an Earth campfire, he thought. Except it isn't Earth. Except it's an alien planet.

There was a rustle in the bushes.

They'll be coming now, he thought. They've figured out that it didn't work. They'll be coming back.

The bushes rustled again and there was the sound of a dislodged stone.

He did not stir.

They can't scare me, he thought. They can't scare —

He felt the breath upon his neck and leaped into the air, spinning as he leaped, stumbling as he came down, almost falling in the fire, then on his feet and scurrying to put the fire between him and the thing that had breathed upon his neck.

He crouched across the fire from it and saw the teeth in the gaping jaws. It raised its head and slashed, as if in pantomime, and he could hear the clicking of the teeth as they came together and the little moaning rumble that came from the massive throat.

A wild thought came to him: It's not an animal at all. This is just part of the gag. Something they dreamed up. If they can build a house like an English wood, use it for a day or two, then cause it to disappear as something for which they have no further use, surely it would be a second's work to dream up an animal.

The animal padded forward and he thought: Animals should be afraid of fire. All animals are afraid of fire. It won't get me if I stay near the fire.

He stooped and grabbed a brand.

Animals are afraid of fire. But this one wasn't. It padded round the fire. It stretched out its neck and sniffed. It wasn't in any hurry, for it was sure of him. Sweat broke out on him and ran down his sides.

The animal came with a smooth rush, whipping around the fire. He leaped, clearing the fire, to gain the other side of it. The animal checked itself, spun around to face him. It put its muzzle to the ground and arched its back. It lashed its tail. It rumbled.

He was frightened now, cold with a fright that could not be laughed off. It might be an animal. It must be an animal. No gag at all, but an animal.

He paced back toward the fire. He danced on his toes, ready to run, to dodge, to fight if he had to fight. But against this thing that faced him across the fire, he knew, there was no fighting chance. And yet, if it came to fighting, he could do no less than fight.

The animal charged.

He ran. He slipped and fell and rolled into the fire.

A hand reached down, jerked him from the fire and flung him to one side, and a voice cried out, a cry of rage and warning.

Then the universe collapsed and he felt himself flying apart and, as suddenly, he was together once again. He lay upon a floor and he scrambled to his feet. His hand was burned and he felt the pain of it. His clothes were smoldering and he beat them out with his uninjured hand.

A voice said, 'I'm sorry, sir. This should not have happened.'

The man was tall, much taller than the Kimonians he had seen before. Nine feet, perhaps. And yet not nine feet, actually. Not anywhere near nine feet. He was no taller, probably, than the taller men of Earth. It was the way he stood that made him seem so tall, the way he stood and looked and the way his voice sounded.

And the first Kimonian, Bishop thought, who had ever shown his age. For there was a silvering of the temple

177

hairs and his face was lined, as the faces of hunters or of sailors are lined from squinting into distances.

They stood facing one another in a room which, when Bishop looked at it, took his breath away. There was no describing it, no way to describe it — you felt as well as saw it. It was a part of you and a part of the universe and a part of everything you'd ever known or dreamed. It seemed to thrust extensions out into unguessed time and space and it had a sense of life and the touch of comfort and the feel of home.

Yet, when he looked again, he sensed a simplicity that did not square with his first impressions. Basic simplicities that tied in with the simple business of living out one's life, as if the room and the folks who lived within its walls were somehow integrated, as if the room were trying its best not to be a room, but to be a part of life, so much a part of life that it could pass unnoticed.

'I was against it from the first,' said the Kimonian. 'Now I know that I was right. But the children wanted you . . .'

'The children?'

'Certainly. I am Elaine's father.'

He didn't say Elaine. He said the other name — the name that Elaine had said no Earthman could pronounce.

'Your hand?' asked the man.

'It's all right,' said Bishop. 'Only burned a little.'

And it was as if he had not spoken, as if he had not said the words — but another man, a man who stood off to one side and spoke the words for him.

He could not have moved if he'd been paid a million.

'This is something,' said the Kimonian, 'that must be recompensed. We'll talk about it later.'

'Please, sir,' said the man who talked for Bishop. 'Please, sir, just one thing. Send me to my hotel.'

He felt the swiftness of the other's understanding — the compassion and the pity.

'Of course,' said the tall man. 'With your permission, sir.'

*

Once there were some children (human children, naturally) who had wanted a dog – a little playful puppy. But their father said they could not have a dog because they would not know how to treat him. But they wanted him so badly and begged their father so much that he finally brought them home a dog, a cunning little puppy, a little butterball with a paunchy belly and four wobbly legs and melting eyes, filled with the innocence of puppyhood.

The children did not treat him so badly as you might have imagined that they would. They were cruel, as all children are. They roughed and tumbled him; they pulled his ears and tail; they teased him. But the pup was full of fun. He liked to play and no matter what they did he came back for more. Because, undoubtedly, he felt very smug in this business of associating with the clever human race, a race so far ahead of dogs in culture and intelligence that there was no comparison at all.

But one day the children went on a picnic and when the day was over they were very tired, and forgetful, as children are very apt to be. So they went off and left the puppy.

That wasn't a bad thing, really. For children will be forgetful, no matter what you do, and the pup was nothing but a dog . . .

The cabinet said, 'You are very late, sir.'

'Yes,' said Bishop dully.

'You hurt somewhere, sir. I can sense the hurt.'

'My hand,' said Bishop. 'I burned it in a fire.'

A panel popped open in the cabinet.

'Put it in there,' said the cabinet. 'I'll fix it in a jiffy.'

Bishop thrust his hand into the opening. He felt finger-like appendages going over it, very gentle and soothing.

'It's not a bad burn, sir,' said the cabinet, 'but I imagine it is painful.'

Playthings, Bishop thought.

This hotel is a dollhouse – or a doghouse. It is a shack, a tacked-together shack like the boys of Earth build out of packing cases and bits of board and paint crude, mystic signs upon. Compared to that room back there it is no more than a hovel, although come to think of it a very gaudy hovel.

Fit for humans, good enough for humans, but a hovel just the same.

And we? he thought. *And we?* The pets of children. The puppy dogs of Kimon. Imported puppy dogs.

'I beg your pardon, sir,' said the cabinet. 'You are not puppy dogs.'

'What's that?'

'You will pardon me, sir. I should not have spoken out. But I wouldn't have wanted you to think – '

'If we aren't pets, what are we?'

'You will excuse me, sir. It was a slip, I quite assure you. I should not have . . .'

'You never do a thing,' said Bishop bitterly, 'without having it all figured out. You or any of them. For you are one of them. You spoke because they wanted you to speak.'

'I can assure you that's not so.'

'You would deny it, naturally,' said Bishop. 'Go ahead and do your job. You haven't told me all they wanted you to tell me. Go ahead and finish.'

'It's immaterial to me what you think,' the cabinet told him. 'But if you thought of yourselves as playmates . . .'

'That's a hot one,' Bishop said.

'Infinitely better,' said the cabinet, 'than thinking of yourself as a puppy dog.'

'So that's what they want me to think.'

'They don't care,' the cabinet said. 'It is all up to you. It was a mere suggestion, sir.'

So, all right, it was a mere suggestion. So, all right, they were playmates and not pets at all.

The kids of Kimon, inviting the dirty, ragged, runny-nosed urchins from across the tracks to play with them. Better to be an invited kid, perhaps, than an imported dog.

But even so it was the children of Kimon who had engineered it all – who had set up the rules for those who wished to come to Kimon, who had built the hotel, had operated it and furnished it with the progressively more

180

luxurious and more enticing rooms, who had found the so-called jobs for humans, who had arranged the printing of the credits.

And if that were so, then it meant that not merely the people of Earth, but the government of Earth, had negotiated, or had attempted to negotiate with the children of another race. And that would be the mark of the difference, he thought, the difference between us.

Although, he told himself, that might not be entirely right.

Maybe he *had* been wrong in thinking, in the first flush of his bitterness, that he was a pet. Maybe he *was* a playmate, an adult Earthman downgraded to the status of a child – and a stupid child at that. Maybe if he had been wrong on the pet angle, he was wrong in the belief, as well, that it had been the children of Kimon who had arranged the immigration of the Earth folk.

And if it hadn't been simply a childish matter of asking in some kids from across the tracks, if the adults of Kimon had had a hand in it, what was the setup then? A school project, a certain phase of progressive education? Or a sort of summer camp project, designed to give the deserving, but underprivileged, Earthmen a vacation away from the squalor of their native planet? Or simply a safe way in which the children of Kimon might amuse and occupy themselves, be kept from underfoot?

We should have guessed it long ago, Bishop told himself. But even if some of us might have entertained the thought that we were either pet or playmate, we should have pushed it far away from us, should have refused to recognize it, for our pride is too tender and too raw for a thought like that.

'There you are, sir,' said the cabinet. 'Almost as good as new. Tomorrow you can take the dressing off.'

He stood before the cabinet without answering. He withdrew his hand and let it fall to his side, like so much dead weight.

Without asking if he wanted it, the cabinet produced a

181

drink. 'I made it long and strong,' said the cabinet. 'I thought you needed it.'

'Thank you,' Bishop said.

He took the drink and stood there with it, not touching it, not wanting to touch it until he'd finished out the thought.

And the thought would not finish out.

There was something wrong. Something that didn't track.

Our pride is too raw and tender – There was something there, some extra words that badly needed saying.

'There is something wrong, sir.'

'Nothing wrong,' said Bishop.

'But your drink.'

'I'll get around to it.'

The Normans had sat their horses on that Saturday afternoon, with the leopard banners curling in the breeze, with the pennons on their lances fluttering, with the sun upon their armor and the scabbards clinking as the horses pranced. They had charged, as history said they had, and had been beaten back. That was entirely right, for it had not been until late afternoon that the Saxon wall was broken, and the final fight around the dragon standard had not taken place until it was nearly dark.

But there had been no Taillefer, riding in the fore to throw up his sword and sing.

On that history had been wrong.

A couple of centuries later, more than likely some copyist had whiled away a monotonous afternoon by writing into the prosaic story of the battle the romance and the glitter of the charge of Taillefer. Writing it in protest against the four blank walls, against his Spartan food, against the daily dullness when spring was in the air and a man should be in the fields or woods instead of shut indoors, hunched with his quills and inkpots.

And that is the way it is with us, thought Bishop. We write the half-truth and the half-lie in our letters home. We conceal a truth or we obscure a fact or we add a line or two that, if not a downright lie, is certainly misleading.

182

We do not face up to facts, he thought. We gloss over the man crawling in the grass, with his torn-out guts snagging on the brambles. We write in the Taillefer.

And if we only did it in our letters, it would not be so bad. But we do it to ourselves. We protect our pride by lying to ourselves. We shield our dignity by deliberate indignation.

'Here,' he said to the cabinet, 'have a drink on me.'

He set the glass, still full, on the top of the cabinet.

The cabinet gurgled in surprise.

'I do not drink,' it said.

'Then take it back and put it in the bottle.'

'I can't do that,' said the cabinet, horrified. 'It's already mixed.'

'Separate it, then.'

'It can't be separated,' wailed the cabinet. 'You surely don't expect me – '

There was a little swish and Maxine stood in the center of the room.

She smiled at Bishop.

'What goes on?' she asked.

The cabinet wailed at her. 'He wants me to unmix a drink. He wants me to separate it, the liquor from the mix. He knows I can't do that.'

'My, my,' she said, 'I thought you could do anything.'

'I can't unravel a drink,' the cabinet said primly. 'Why don't you take it off my hands?'

'That's a good idea,' said the girl. She walked forward and picked up the drink.

'What's wrong with you?' she asked Bishop. 'Turning chicken on us?'

'I just don't want a drink,' said Bishop. 'Hasn't a man got a right to – ?'

'Of course,' she said. 'Of course you have.'

She sipped the drink, looking at him above the rim.

'What happened to your hand?'

'Burned it.'

'You're old enough not to play with fire.'

'You're old enough not to come barging into a room this

way,' Bishop told her. 'One of these days you'll reassemble yourself in the precise spot where someone else is standing.'

She giggled. 'That would be fun,' she said. 'Think of you and me . . .'

'It would be a mess,' said Bishop.

'Invite me to sit down,' said Maxine. 'Let's act civilized and social.'

'Sure, sit down,' said Bishop.

She picked out a couch.

'I'm interested in this business of teleporting yourself,' said Bishop. 'I've asked you before, but you never told me.'

'It just came to me,' she said.

'But you can't teleport. Humans aren't parapsychic – '

'Some day, buster, you'll blow a fuse. You get so steamed up.'

He went across the room and sat down beside her.

'Sure, I get steamed up,' he said. 'But . . .'

'What now?'

'Have you ever thought – well, have you ever tried to work at it? Like moving something else, some object – other than yourself?'

'No, I never have.'

'Why not?'

'Look, buster. I drop in to have a drink with you and to forget myself. I didn't come primed for a long technical discussion. I couldn't anyway. I just don't understand. There's so much we don't understand.'

She looked at him and there was something very much like fright brimming in her eyes.

'You pretend that you don't mind,' she said. 'But you do mind. You wear yourself out pretending that you don't mind at all.'

'Then let's quit pretending,' Bishop said. 'Let's admit . . .'

She had lifted the glass to drink and now, suddenly it slipped out of her hand.

'Oh – '

184

The glass halted before it struck the floor. It hovered for a moment, then it slowly rose. She reached out and grasped it.

And then it slipped again from her suddenly shaking hand. This time it hit the floor and spilled.

'Try it again,' said Bishop.

She said, 'I never tried. I don't know how it happened. I just didn't want to drop it, that was all. I wished I hadn't dropped it and then . . .'

'But the second time – '

'You fool,' she screamed, 'I tell you I didn't try. I wasn't putting on an exhibition for you. I tell you that I don't know what happened.'

'But you did it. It was a start.'

'A start?'

'You caught the glass before it hit the floor. You teleported it back into your hand.'

'Look, buster,' she said grimly, 'quit kidding yourself. They're watching all the time. They play little tricks like that. Anything for a laugh.'

She rose, laughing at him, but there was a strangeness in her laughing.

'You don't give yourself a chance,' he told her. 'You are so horribly afraid of being laughed at. You've got to be a wise guy.'

'Thanks for the drink,' she said.

'But Maxine – '

'Come up and see me sometime.'

'Maxine! Wait!'

But she was gone.

Watch for the clues, Morley had said, pacing up and down the room. Send us back the clues and we will do the rest. A foot in the door is all we expect from you. Give us a foot inside the door and that is all we need.

Clues, he had said. Not fact, but clues.

And perhaps he had said clues instead of facts because he had been blinded like all the rest of them. Like the copyist who could not face up to the fact of battle without chivalry. Like those who wrote the letters home from Kimon. Like Maxine, who said quit kidding yourself, buster, they're watching all the time; they play little tricks like this.

And here were facts.

Facts he should send home to Morley. Except he couldn't send them.

He was ashamed to send them.

You couldn't write: *We are pets. The children house and feed us. They throw sticks for us to chase. They like to hear us bark* . . . He sweated as he thought of it.

Or the kinder fact: *We are playmates* . . .

You couldn't write that, either. You simply couldn't write it.

And yet, he said, the facts are there – the truth is there. And you must admit it. You must admit the fact. And you must admit the truth. If not for Morley, if not for Earth, if not for fellow man, then you must admit it for yourself. For a man may fool his friends, he may deceive the world – but he must be truthful with himself. Let's forget the bitterness, he told himself – the bitterness and hurt. Let's forget the pride.

Let us look for facts.

The Kimonians are a race more culturally advanced than we are, which means, in other words, that they are farther along the road of evolution, farther from the ape. And what does it take to advance along the evolutionary road beyond the high tide of my own race of Earth?

Not mere intelligence alone, for that is not enough.

What then would it take to make the next major stride in evolution? Perhaps philosophy rather than intelligence – a seeking for a way to put to better use the intelligence that one already had, a greater understanding and a more adequate appreciation of human values in relation to the universe.

And if the Kimonians had that greater understanding, if they had won their way through better understanding to closer brotherhood with the galaxy, then it would be inconceivable that they'd take the members of another

186

intelligent race to serve as puppy dogs for children. Or even as playmates for their children, unless in the fact of playing with their children there be some greater value, not to the child alone, but to the child of Earth, than the happiness and wonder of such association. They would be alive to the psychic damage that might be done because of such a practice, would not for a moment run the danger of that damage happening unless out of it might come some improvement or some change.

He sat and thought of it and it seemed right, for even on his native planet history showed increasing concern with social values as the culture improved.

And something else.

Parapsychic powers must not come too soon in human evolution, for they could be used disastrously by a culture that was not equipped, emotionally and intelligently, to handle them. No culture which had not reached an adult stage could have parapsychic powers, for they were nothing to be fooled around with by an adolescent culture.

In that respect at least, Bishop told himself, the Kimonians are the adults and we are the adolescents. In comparison with the Kimonians, we have no right to consider ourselves any more than children.

It was hard to take. He gagged on it. Swallow it, he told himself. Swallow it.

The cabinet said, 'It is late, sir. You must be getting tired.'

'You want me to go to bed?'

'It's a suggestion, sir.'

'All right,' he said.

He rose and started for the bedroom, smiling to himself. Sent off to bed, he thought – just as a child is sent. And going.

Not saying, 'I'll go when I'm ready.' Not standing on your adult dignity. Not throwing a tantrum, not beating your heels upon the floor and howling.

Going off to bed – like a child when it's told to go.

Maybe that's the way, he thought. Maybe that's the answer. Maybe that's the *only* answer.

He swung around.

'Cabinet.'

'What is it, sir?'

'Nothing,' Bishop said. 'Nothing at all . . . that is. Thanks for fixing up my hand.'

'That's quite all right,' said the cabinet. 'Good night.'

Maybe that's the answer. To act like a child. And what does a child do? He goes to bed when he is told. He minds his elders. He goes to school. He – Wait a minute!

He goes to school!

He goes to school because there is a lot to learn. He goes to kindergarten so that he can get into the first grade and he goes to high school so that he can go to college. He realizes there is a lot to learn, that before he takes his place in the adult world it must be learned and that he has to work to learn.

But I went to school, Bishop told himself. I went for years and years. I studied hard and I passed an examination that a thousand others failed to pass. I qualified for Kimon.

But just suppose.

You went to kindergarten to qualify for first grade. You went to high school to qualify for college. You went to Earth to qualify for Kimon.

You might have a doctorate on Earth, but still be no more than a kindergarten youngster when you got to Kimon.

Monty knew a bit of telepathy and so did some of the others. Maxine could teleport herself and she had made the glass stop before it hit the floor. Perhaps the others could, too.

And they'd just picked it up.

Although just telepathy or stopping a glass from hitting the floor would not be all of it. There'd be much more of it. Much more to the culture of Kimon than the parapsychic arts.

Maybe we are ready, he thought. Maybe we've almost finished with our adolescence. Maybe we are on the verge of being ready for an adult culture. Could that be why the

Kimonians let us in, the only ones in the galaxy they are willing to let in?

His brain reeled with the thought.

On Earth only one of every thousand passed the examination that sent them on to Kimon. Maybe here on Kimon only another one in every thousand would be qualified to absorb the culture that Kimon offered them.

But before you could even start to absorb the culture, before you could start to learn, before you ever went to school, you'd have to admit that you didn't know. You'd have to admit that you were a child. You couldn't go on having tantrums. You couldn't be a wise guy. You couldn't keep on polishing up false pride to hold as a shield between you and the culture that waited for your understanding.

Morley, Bishop said, I may have the answer – the answer that you're awaiting back on Earth.

But I can't tell it to you. It's something that can't be told. It's a thing that each one must find out for himself.

And the pity of it is that Earth is not really equipped to find it out. It is not a lesson that is often taught on Earth.

Armies and guns could not storm the citadel of Kimonian culture, for you simply could not fight a war with a parapsychic people. Earth aggressiveness and business cunning likewise would fail to crack the dead-pan face of Kimon.

There is only one way, Morley, Bishop said, talking to his friend. There is only one thing that will crack this planet and that is humility. And Earthmen are not humble creatures. Long ago they forgot the meaning of humility. But here it's different. Here you have to be different.

You start out by saying, I don't know. Then you say, I want to know. Then you say, I'll work hard to learn.

Maybe, Bishop thought, that's why they brought us here, so that the one of us in every thousand who has a chance of learning would get that chance to learn. Maybe they are watching, hoping that there may be more than one in every thousand. Maybe they are more anxious for us to learn than we are to learn. For they may be lonely in a galaxy where there are no others like them.

189

Could it be that the ones at this hotel were the failures, the ones who had never tried, or who might have tried and could not pass.

And the others – the one out of every thousand – where were they? He could not even guess.

There were no answers. It was all supposition. It was a premise built upon a pipedream – built on wishful thinking. He would wake up in the morning and know that it was wrong.

He'd go down to the bar and have a drink with Maxine or with Monty and laugh at himself for the things that he'd dreamed up.

School, he'd told himself. But it wouldn't be a school – at least not the kind of school he'd ever known before.

I wish it could be so, he thought.

The cabinet said, 'You'd better get on to bed, sir.'

'I suppose I should,' said Bishop. 'It's been a long, hard day.'

'You'll want to get up early,' said the cabinet, 'so you aren't late to school.'

A Selected List of Science Fiction Available from Mandarin

While every effort is made to keep prices low, it is sometimes necessary to increase prices at short notice. Mandarin Paperbacks reserves the right to show new retail prices on covers which may differ from those previously advertised in the text or elsewhere.

The prices shown below were correct at the time of going to press.

☐	7493 0021 3	**Kinsman**	Ben Bova	£3.50
☐	7493 0083 8	**Millennium**	Ben Bova	£3.50
☐	7493 0120 1	**Peacekeepers**	Ben Bova	£3.50
☐	7493 0105 8	**The Compleat Traveller in Black**	John Brunner	£3.50
☐	7493 0007 8	**The Chronicles of Morgaine**	C. J. Cherryh	£4.99
☐	7493 0154 6	**Downbelow Station**	C. J. Cherryh	£3.99
☐	7493 0006 X	**Exile's Gate**	C. J. Cherryh	£3.99
☐	7493 0068 X	**Pride of Chanur**	C. J. Cherryh	£2.99
☐	7493 0100 7	**Serpents Reach**	C. J. Cherryh	£3.50
☐	7493 0038 8	**Highway of Eternity**	Clifford D. Simak	£2.99
☐	7493 0099 X	**Off-Planet**	Clifford D. Simak	£3.50
☐	7493 0079 5	**Where the Evil Dwells**	Clifford D. Simak	£3.50
☐	7493 0103 1	**Deep Space**	Eric Frank Russell	£2.99
☐	7493 0047 7	**A Splendid Chaos**	John Shirley	£3.99
☐	7493 0037 X	**Ravenmoon**	Peter Tremayne	£3.50

All these books are available at your bookshop or newsagent, or can be ordered direct from the publisher. Just tick the titles you want and fill in the form below.

Mandarin Paperbacks, Cash Sales Department, PO Box 11, Falmouth, Cornwall TR10 9EN.

Please send cheque or postal order, no currency, for purchase price quoted and allow the following for postage and packing:

UK	80p for the first book, 20p for each additional book ordered to a maximum charge of £2.00.
BFPO	80p for the first book, 20p for each additional book.
Overseas including Eire	£1.50 for the first book, £1.00 for the second and 30p for each additional book thereafter.

NAME (Block letters) ....

ADDRESS ....

....

....